Hearts Unfrozen

MEN OF MELBOURNE, Volume 3

Alex Leslie

Published by Alex Leslie, 2022.

HEARTS UNFROZEN

First edition. March 1, 2022.

Copyright © 2022 Alex Leslie.

ISBN: 979-8201422363

Written by Alex Leslie.

Table of Contents

Prologue

"YOU'RE BEING COMPLETELY IRRATIONAL!" Paul Kincaid growled, as he desperately tried and failed to contain his temper. He watched as his equally enraged boyfriend dashed around Paul's house, collecting the few personal items Justin had left there during previous visits and shoving them into his backpack.

When Paul had texted Justin a few hours ago and asked him to meet him at his house, he was hoping things would go very differently. He had expected that the news he had been excited to share with his boyfriend would provoke a reaction that was a bit more happy and uplifting than the psychotic tantrum he was currently witnessing.

"Irrational?!" Justin spat back with righteous indignation, "You just don't get it, do you? You tell me you have good news, that you've been promoted to Homicide. Then you tell me you're likely to be working even more hours than you are already, and you expect me to what? Celebrate? Are you really that obtuse?"

Apparently, Paul was that obtuse. He had foolishly assumed that his boyfriend would be happy and supportive that Paul had finally managed to score the long sought after promotion he'd been recently working his arse off to secure. He'd believed that Justin would want to congratulate him on a job well done, and celebrate his success with a night on the town. But apparently, the news that a higher position on the Police force came with longer, more unpredictable working hours and increased responsibilities had shattered all of Justin's long-held illusions of what going out with a cop was really like.

"What's the point of dating a cop if I never get to see you?" Justin was near apoplectic, "You don't even wear a uniform, so what's the fucking point?"

And all of a sudden, it was like a fog had lifted. In that instant, Paul could see Justin for what he truly was. It wasn't entirely a surprise. Justin had made no secret that he had a fetish for cops. He was your typical badge bunny who got hot for handcuffs, getting taken 'downtown' and, of course, the uniform.

Paul didn't initially care about that. He had hoped that the two of them would develop something more, something deeper, something beyond kinky fun in the bedroom. But as the weeks rolled on, and Paul had become busier and busier at work, Justin had become angrier and angrier. Justin seemed to live in a fantasy land where cops worked nine to five jobs and could pick and choose their workdays. He never understood why Paul couldn't just drop everything to meet Justin and his friends at a nightclub or bar. Justin would become frustrated when plans were made, but then got canceled at the last minute because his work schedule had undergone an unexpected change. Paul hoped that Justin would eventually come to understand that Paul's work wasn't like Justin's office job. But clearly, that had not happened.

"Sounds to me like you're more interested in dating a cop than you are in dating me," Paul said with quiet resignation. His anger had melted away, replaced with a melancholy realisation. This wasn't his first rodeo. He knew what was coming next.

Justin stopped and looked at him. For a moment, Justin seemed almost confused by Paul's statement. But as he buckled up his backpack and grabbed his keys off the coffee table, Paul could see the resolve etched on his face. The axe was about to fall.

"I'm sorry, but this isn't what I signed on for. I thought we were going to have some fun, go out, see where things went. But in two months I've barely seen you four times, and most of the time it was just us watching a movie on the couch after one of your long shifts. And sitting around watching you crash out five minutes into a movie does not a relationship make."

With that, Justin grabbed his backpack and strode out the door, leaving Paul alone in his silent, empty house. In that moment, Paul figured he should chase after Justin. Try to convince him to stay. Maybe work things out. But he knew in his heart there was no point. Justin was handsome, fun, and great in the sack – but he wasn't cut out to be a cop's partner.

So Paul just stood there, rooted to the spot in the middle of the living room. The house, which Paul had inherited from his beloved Grandfather, that was usually filled with the warmth and memories that always brought him comfort, suddenly felt cold and desolate. Like all the life and joy had just been unceremoniously sucked out of his home as Justin departed. He shook his head at the thought. It wasn't like Justin had been the love of his life. In reality, Paul barely knew the man. But Justin had represented Paul's hope of Mr. Right. The man of his dreams. A partner in life to come home to each night and share everything with.

But as Paul looked around at the metaphorical smoldering wreckage that was yet another unsuccessful relationship, it dawned on him that perhaps there was a reason so many police officers ended up living solitary, romance-free lives. The demands of a cop's partner were extreme. They have to learn to accept a life of always being put on the back burner; knowing the job would always have to come first. They had to accept the long, ever-changing, unpredictable shifts, and the lack of free time. But most of all, they had to accept the emotionally draining realisation that for some cops, each shift could be their last. That one day, they could get that dreaded phone call or knock at the door, telling them that their loved one was never coming home.

Paul had suffered through more than his fair share of failed relationships; and while he and Justin hadn't been seeing each other long, it still hurt knowing he had, once again, failed to find someone to love. It was beginning to look like finding that one true love and soulmate was simply something other people got to do.

It was then that Paul decided that the time had come to accept the inevitable. He was never going to find Mr. Right. That he should stop wasting his time trying to find someone that could live with his schedule and was emotionally mature enough to cope with life as a cop's partner. It was time to accept he was destined to spend his life alone.

Chapter 1

IF JAROD CRUIKSHANK was capable of being frustrated, he would certainly be frustrated right now. Translating books written in Hungarian wasn't an easy task at the best of times. But being asked to translate a complicated operation and maintenance manual, for what appeared to be some kind of ancient Hungarian combine harvester, was starting to test even his unshakable calm.

Jarod knew nothing about farming, knew even less about farm equipment, and, while he was a talented linguist whose skills in translating the written word were as remarkable as they were highly sought after, Hungarian was not one of his strongest languages.

I can't be good at everything.

Normally, he wouldn't take on such a complicated project if his knowledge of the subject matter was lacking, especially when the client required the translation to be completed at short notice. But since his client needed it as quickly as humanly possible, and was willing to pay a simply extraordinary amount of money to get it done, Jarod had reluctantly agreed to take on the job. As an independent freelancer working from home, he couldn't afford to turn down such a lucrative offer. This one translation would keep all his bills paid for a considerably long time.

He had already spent two whole days working on this project, and at this point, his brain felt like it was turning to mush. But his perseverance with the nearly incomprehensible text had eventually paid off, and after a few hours, Jarod managed to get into the swing of things. Despite the technical terms and Hungarian farming jargon that was borderline meaningless to anyone outside of Budapest, he was able to get enough of the text translated that he only needed to spend a short time looking up and translating a few stubborn words and phrases from his notes or a few reliable online reference sites.

Jarod had been granted a natural gift for the written word ever since early childhood. But his memory could only retain so much information. As an aid to recall, Jarod kept extensive handwritten notes on each language he had experience with, especially with the more complicated ones he rarely had to work with. The result was shelf after shelf of notebooks stored on the various bookshelves around his apartment.

His 'office' was mostly just a work desk situated by the living room windows, bookended by large, dominating wooden shelving units. In fact, almost every wall in the living room had bookshelves. The spare bedroom had been converted into a library for Jarod's extensive classic book collection when he moved into the apartment six years ago. However, it didn't take long for the collection to start overflowing into the rest of his home, necessitating the installation of additional shelves.

Jarod was all too aware that his constantly expanding book collection was quickly getting out of control. Besides his language notebooks, Jarod collected fiction and non-fiction books in a variety of languages. Some were reference books from his time at the university, which he kept as they aided with his translation work. Others were simply books he had, once upon a time, loved and enjoyed getting lost in. Jarod mostly kept those books out of whatever he had left that passed for a sense of sentimentality, although he did still find it relaxing to grab a random book and let the words flow over him. One of these days, Jarod would have to accept the inevitable and find a larger home to accommodate him and his ever-growing forest of bookshelves.

Located in the heart of Northcote, a quiet northern suburb of Melbourne, Jarod's apartment building – The Paradiso – was a classic example of the type of grand Art Deco-style homes that had been popular in the area back in the day. Once a small hotel, the building had subsequently been subdivided into six separate apartments over three floors. Along with Jarod's second-floor apartment, The Paradiso was home to an eclectic collection of tenants that he usually tried not to interact with unless absolutely necessary.

The last thing I need is to offend one of my neighbours, and get kicked out of my home, too.

It was well after lunchtime before Jarod decided to take a break from all things Hungarian. The translation was mostly complete. All that was left was a couple of edits, a bit of polishing, and then it could be emailed through to the client. While Jarod wasn't frustrated per se with the slow progress on his latest project, he was filled with a certain degree of tension. Jarod briefly wondered how bad it would be if he were actually capable of experiencing true frustration. Jarod stepped away from his desk, stretched for a few seconds, crossed the living room, and entered the kitchen. He switched on the electric kettle and began preparing a mug of Camomile tea.

Three years earlier, Jarod had been involved in a car accident on his way home from a day of lecturing at the Melbourne City University. The roads were bustling with peak hour traffic and the rain had been atrocious. As he was driving through a busy intersection, a careless driver in a stolen car had run a red light and slammed straight into the driver's side of Jarod's vehicle. Unfortunately, the driver fled the scene before anyone could stop them, so they were never identified. Jarod had been rushed to hospital with serious head injuries, but during emergency surgery, he had experienced a stroke.

It had taken months for Jarod to recover from the accident, but the stroke had left him with permanent neurological damage. While he had eventually regained his pre-injury speech and motor skills, the doctors had quickly realised his brain injury had left Jarod unable to experience or process emotions. Jarod was a 'blank slate' for lack of a better phrase. He didn't feel things deeply like he once had, and frequently had problems identifying emotions in other people. Without feelings, Jarod had instantly been transformed into an entirely different person.

He had initially felt no ill effects from his new state of being. Relieved of his emotions, Jarod was no longer affected by depression, stress, or anxiety. He no longer felt lonely or frustrated. He wasn't distracted by infatuations or heartbreaks. He just... existed.

Thanks to Australia's free public health system, Jarod wasn't left with any expensive medical bills, plus the generous life insurance policy that came with his employment meant that, regardless of what happened going forward, he would be able to cover his cost of living expenses indefinitely. However, Jarod fully intended to return to work as soon as possible. He didn't like the idea of sitting idle when he was still capable of doing what he did best.

Being a university lecturer, bookworm, and lifelong nerd, anxiety was something he had dealt with for years. To be suddenly free of it, unencumbered by its ability to control his life, Jarod almost saw his neurological changes as a blessing in disguise. He would be able to focus on his work without getting stressed out, therefore making him more productive. He would no longer get nervous while performing lectures. This could be the best thing that ever happened to him.

But it didn't take long to discover his new persona was not quite the jackpot win he had envisaged. While he was certainly no longer capable of feeling stressed or anxious, he also seemed incapable of censoring himself in any given situation. Whatever random ideas crossed his mind, no matter how inappropriate, would come blurting out of his mouth without a second thought. This lead to many problems at the university, when his students and fellow faculty members became frustrated with his outspoken behaviour.

And Jarod *was* outspoken – all the time. Sometimes his internal monologues were not that internal. And it seemed people didn't appreciate him blatantly stating how awful he thought their clothes were. Nor would he shy away from telling people if they were boring him. That one, in particular, didn't go down well with his superiors.

Worse still, Jarod didn't really understand what all the fuss was about. It wasn't like what he was saying were lies. Surely Professor Maxwell would want to know his knitted pullover looked like diarrhoea? Shouldn't Donna Crawford in the front row of Jarod's Wednesday lecture be grateful someone would point out to her that she needed a stronger, better-performing brand of deodorant? Wasn't it appropriate to be truthful? Apparently not all the time, it wasn't.

Eventually, he was placed on administrative leave while the university conducted an investigation into his behaviour. Jarod didn't really understand what he had done wrong, but he didn't object to taking some time off. That's when Caroline stepped in.

His older sister, upon hearing what had happened at the university, immediately flew down from Sydney to take charge of the situation. Jarod wasn't sure why she would do that, but any attempt to dissuade her was met with her stone-cold resolve. After consulting both with Jarod's doctors and the university administrators, she eventually convinced him that it was essential that Jarod fly back to Sydney with her while they worked on getting him some kind of treatment. Caroline was convinced that Jarod just needed to get some more doctors involved; that someone out there would have a solution to her brother's unusual malady.

However, after months of seeing specialist after specialist, Jarod had to come to accept that while the remote possibility existed that his brain may someday 're-wire' itself and regain some of it's lost neurological function, all the specialists agreed this was a highly unlikely scenario. Caroline strongly disagreed. She insisted that Western medicine did not have all the answers and that they should begin exploring non-traditional medical options. Jarod indulged his sister initially, but he didn't see the point of wasting time consulting with faith healers, crystal practitioners, or other such nonsense. He just wanted to go back to work and live his life, so Jarod returned to

Melbourne, over Caroline's objections, and had remained there ever since.

After their investigation was complete, the university had given Jarod two options: take early retirement, or get fired. Jarod elected to take the early retirement option and decided immediately that he would work from home as a freelance book and text translator. It wouldn't cost much to set up as a business; he could work from the comfort of his apartment where he wouldn't accidentally upset anyone; and he would be doing something useful with his skills rather than vegetating away eating goji berries and exploring his chakras with his sister's happy-clapping, hippy con artists.

After his forced retirement, Caroline tried to use his dismissal as proof that Jarod needed to come back to Sydney. She insisted that he could no longer live on his own; that he needed a full-time carer since apparently, he couldn't take care of himself. Jarod dismissed his sister's objections without a second thought. Aside from the interpersonal issues he had experienced at the university, he had been perfectly capable of looking after his daily needs. His sister was, as usual when she didn't get her way, exaggerating the problem so she could regain the upper hand. Jarod remembered this from their childhood. If it looked like his sister was losing an argument, she would simply make up some story and stick to it until everyone just ended up agreeing with her to shut her up. But Jarod wasn't going to do that this time. His life was in Melbourne, and it had been for years. He wasn't going to be nursemaided by his sister or anyone else.

Jarod was broken from his trip down memory lane by the whistling of the kettle. He poured the boiling water into the prepared mug and brought it over to the dining table. The mug had an image of a dancing avocado on it. A vulgar souvenir his sister had sent him from some tourist trap she visited on her last holiday to Queensland. Apparently 'Avocado Land' had been downright 'craptastic' (in his sister's words) and Caroline had hoped Jarod would find the coffee mug 'cute'. Jarod mostly felt that despite its unaesthetic visage, it was the perfect size for his afternoon cup of tea, so had kept it to perform that function.

Jarod quietly sipped the herbal brew as he tried to *not* think about Hungarian farm equipment for a little while. It was then he noticed the bulky book on Ancient Egypt that he had placed on the dining table late last night. He had dug it out of his vast book collection at the request of his elderly neighbour. Clarissa, the one person at The Paradiso he regularly interacted with (since she had long ago demonstrated she was not easily offended by Jarod's occasional bluntness) had asked if he had a book her Grandson could borrow to aid in reproducing realistic Egyptian hieroglyphics for a school project. Jarod had several books on the subject, but this one was likely to be the most accessible for a child. It had lots of colourful pictures that would appeal to a young mind.

Jarod found it interesting that his interactions with his neighbour had significantly improved since the accident. The elderly widow had been a source of endless frustration for him before his brain injury, as she was forever knocking on his door to inform him about the latest gossipy minutiae of their fellow neighbours, people at the senior's centre she frequented and popular culture figures he'd never heard of – none of which even remotely interested Jarod in the slightest. The daily visits had become something of an annoyance, but post-accident had become something he has able to tolerate without issue.

It was then he realised that Clarissa had not yet interrupted his day. Usually, she would briefly visit in the morning on her way out to the Senior's Centre, asking if Jarod needed anything from the shops on her way home. But today, Clarissa had been strangely absent.

Maybe I just didn't notice her knocking on the door?

This was a distinct possibility. One of the reasons he was forced to hire a part-time assistant was that he frequently got so wrapped up in his work, the rest of the world would more or less melt away. Good from a productivity standpoint, but not so great if he forgot to do his laundry or pay the electricity bill. Troy Merrick, a student from the university, would come over a few times a week to do some light housekeeping and help with the day-to-day administration of his home business. Today was Troy's day off, but usually, it would be Troy who would see to things like doing Jarod's laundry, making tea, or answering doors.

That being said, Jarod hadn't experienced the kind of laser focus today that would allow himself to ignore a knock at his front door, so he dismissed the possibility. Clarissa had said yesterday she would be around first thing in the morning to collect the book. Looking at the clock on the wall, Jarod noted it was well after one pm. While she may be getting on in years, Clarissa's mind was still sharp as a tack. It was highly unlikely she would have simply forgotten, especially when the book was for her Grandson. The old woman was forever doting on the young boy.

Finishing his tea, Jarod picked up the book in question, grabbed his phone and keys, then proceeded out the front door. Clarissa lived in the apartment across the hall, and Jarod had been given a set of her keys many years ago in case of an emergency. While he wasn't expecting an emergency, he figured it would be wise to check on his neighbour. She had suffered a bad chest cold last winter, but stubborn as a mule, she refused to seek medical assistance until Jarod came over to check on her.

Just as Jarod was locking his front door, he heard the now-familiar approach of clunking footsteps on the staircase. His upstairs neighbour, Barry, had moved in a couple of years ago and was one of those men who didn't 'believe' in things like deodorant or soap. He believed the body naturally took care of itself, and that using such 'poisons' was little more than buying a first-class ticket to an early grave. In the real world, Barry smelled like a ripe compost heap, frequently had horrendously dirty fingernails, and hair so greasy and unkempt that Jarod thought it looked more like a poorly engineered bird's nest. Despite Jarod's barren emotional state, Barry, or at least his objectionable hygiene practices, was one of the few things on Earth that could trigger a deep, visceral reaction within him.

Despite his general foulness and unappealing presentation, Barry staggeringly considered himself God's gift to gay men and would flirt outrageously with Jarod at any given opportunity. The idea of being in close proximity to that man was nothing short of stomach-churning, let alone having any kind of sexual interaction with him. The idea was just too unhygienic for Jarod to comprehend, and the very thought made him feel queasy.

Jarod quickly dashed across the hall to Clarissa's front door and fumbled with his key ring, trying to find the correct key as fast as possible. Barry stopped at the top of the stairs, spotted Jarod immediately, and smiled toothily like some deep-sea predator that had spotted a lone and isolated prey animal.

Shit.

"Morning, Barry! Sorry, I can't stop and chat. Clarissa is expecting me. Have a nice day!" Jarod stammered as he unlocked the door and dashed inside. Before Barry could even respond, Jarod closed and locked the door behind him, and briefly considered barricading the entryway. He took a few deep, cleansing breaths to dispel the overpowering Barry funk from his palate and dislodged the moist aroma from his nasal passages. Hopefully, Barry would be gone by the time Jarod needed to return to his apartment.

Jarod placed the heavy book about Ancient Egypt on Clarissa's entry table, in a prominent position she was unlikely to miss. He turned away from the front door, walked down the short hallway, and entered the living room. He immediately stopped and took in the scene before him.

The living room was in total disarray. The place looked like it had been hit by a cyclone. Clarissa's antique mahogany magazine rack had been knocked over, the contents spilled all over the floor. The glass coffee table was smashed, with shards scattered everywhere, and his neighbour's favourite comfy chair had been tipped over onto its side. The wall directly opposite the front door was covered with a significant quantity of blood. Amongst the spray and splatter marks were what appeared to be some kind of symbols written directly onto Clarissa's gorgeous Old Country Roses themed wallpaper.

Well, this is dreadful! Clarissa is not going to be impressed when she sees all this mess.

Looking down at the ground under the macabre finger paintings, Jarod spotted Clarissa's prone and bloodied corpse. She had been brutally murdered. Beside her body lay a large kitchen knife that was stained with blood. Jarod presumed this was the murder weapon.

So that's why she didn't come over and collect the book. I knew there had to be a logical reason.

Jarod pulled his phone out of his pocket and promptly called Emergency Services.

"Emergency Triple Zero. What service do you require?"

"Um, Good question. I'm not sure if this qualifies as an emergency, but I wasn't sure who else to call. Obviously, the police will be required, but do the Ambulance Service deal with dead bodies? Or are they strictly an 'alive people only' sort of service?"

"Sir, did you say... dead bodies?"

"Yes. Well, I say 'bodies' - there's only the one as far as I know. My elderly neighbour is dead. So could you please send over whoever you think it best to deal with such a situation?"

"Sir, are you certain your neighbour is actually dead?"

"Well. she's been stabbed multiple times, partially decapitated and most of her blood is on the walls and floor, so I'm fairly confident she's won't be cashing her pension cheque this fortnight."

The line went silent. Jarod thought the call had been disconnected, but checking the screen revealed the call was apparently still active.

Jarod needed to invest in a better phone. He idly considered the options.

"Okay, sir. I need to get some information from you. Can you tell me your address?"

Oh, good. The phone is working. Replacing it would be an unexpected expense I could live without.

Jarod gave the operator the required information and was informed that Emergency personnel were being dispatched immediately. The operator asked Jarod to wait outside the apartment in the hallway. Jarod agreed reluctantly, remembering Barry may still be lurking, then ended the call.

Stepping gingerly out into the hallway, Jarod saw no sign of his offensive neighbour, but his scent still hung heavily in the air. He wondered if he had time to go into his own apartment and retrieve the can of air freshener from the bathroom. He decided to wait until the police, or whoever was coming, arrived. Within a few minutes, a pair of paramedics were first on the scene and Jarod directed them into Clarissa's apartment. Soon the whole building was filled with emergency personnel from various departments and agencies. Jarod was asked by a uniformed police officer to take a seat inside his apartment while they established an official crime scene and await the arrival of the detectives assigned to the case.

Chapter 2

PAUL HAD BEEN at the Northcote crime scene for over an hour, looking through the blood-splattered apartment for clues, as the forensics team photographed everything. Eventually, they had images of the whole scene and the victim's body could finally be removed.

As the elderly lady was zipped into a body bag and transported away on a gurney, Paul examined the bloody writing on the living room wall. 'Writing' was probably not the correct word for the grotesque finger paintings. They were more like symbols. Angular and jagged, formed from various horizontal and vertical lines. He hadn't seen anything like them before, and Paul couldn't see any meaningful pattern to them. The killer had clearly spent some time transcribing the symbols onto the wall and had apparently used the victim's own blood, so they clearly carried some meaning. But whether it was simply part of the killer's fantasy or ritual; a way of unnerving the police or perhaps the victim's family; or if the cryptic symbols did actually convey some specific message was yet to be determined.

Paul was exhausted. The last few months had been draining. Getting settled in his new role at Homicide; the long, arduous hours; the lack of sleep and the daily knowledge that he would be going home to an empty, lonely house was beginning to take its toll. He had tried to accept that he was better off without the complications a romantic relationship could bring, but his solitude was beginning to get to him.

Shaking himself out of his troubling thoughts, he focused on his investigation of the apartment. On the entry table by the door, Paul noticed a large, heavy book about Ancient Egypt. Given than the victim didn't appear to have any similar books elsewhere in the apartment, the book stood out like a sore thumb.

Were the symbols Egyptian? Did the killer leave the book here? Why? Is it a clue? A taunt? A red herring?

Returning to the living room, Paul tried to get a sense of who the victim was. Victimology is important in murder investigations as, in many cases, the victim and their killer frequently have some kind of connection. Finding out everything you can about the victim can sometimes lead you directly to the guilty party.

While Paul had only been in Homicide for a few months, he had been a detective with the Melbourne City Police for over a decade. But nothing in his experience remotely compared to the crime scene before him. He hoped his partner, who was currently giving testimony in an unrelated court case, would have some insight into the symbols and to why a seemingly harmless, little old lady would be the victim of such a savage, brutal attack.

As if on cue, Detective Bryce Gordon lumbered into the apartment. The formal navy blue suit, which the man only ever wore when he was in court, was stretched over his enormous muscular frame to the point that Paul was surprised the fabric didn't rip at the seams. While Paul was a fit and muscular man himself, Bryce dwarfed him in both height and bulk. His imposing appearance was made all the more intimidating by the permanent resting scowl that adorned the man's face.

"Sorry, I'm late. Traffic from the courthouse was a bitch. So, what have we got?"

Paul smirked. He knew how much his partner hated making court appearances, even though they were a regular part of any detective's job. Almost as much as Bryce hated having to wear his formal suit whenever he was expected to attend court. Paul retrieved his notebook from his pocket and flipped it open to his notes on the case so far.

"Clarissa Wainwright, 78; retired widow, lived here alone. Medical Examiner reports she was stabbed approximately twenty-five times; throat slashed; the victim's blood has been used by the killer to draw symbols of some kind on the wall."

"God almighty." Bryce took in the scene. "Any witnesses?"

"Not so far. The victim was discovered by a neighbour, Jarod Cruickshank, in the apartment next door. He was the one who called it in. The Triple Zero operator reported Cruickshank was a little unusual on the phone; oddly calm, slightly abrupt, but the operator put it down to shock. I haven't questioned him yet. He's across the hall in his apartment. I put a uniform on guard at his door to keep an eye on him, just in case."

"I listened to the recording of the call on my way over here. The guy sounds like a fuckin' creep. My money's on him being our guy."

With that, Bryce moved to the far wall to look at the blood splatter and the hand-drawn message. Paul shook his head.

Bryce was a good cop, but sometimes he would form an opinion based on very little evidence, and nothing short of a stick of dynamite would force him to change his mind.

Paul watched as his partner used his phone camera to take close up shots of some of the symbols. He used the phone screen to zoom in on the images, examining the finest details.

"No fingerprints on the finger paintings. The killer must have been wearing gloves when he drew them." Bryce muttered to himself, not looking away from the image on the phone screen.

Damn. A killer who was using forensic countermeasures. The case just got a little harder to solve.

"What about this... writing? Do you recognise it?" Bryce asked, turning his attention back to Paul.

"Doesn't mean anything to me. But there was a book on Ancient Egypt on the hallway table. It looked out of place so I had it taken it into evidence. It might have been left by our suspect."

The two detectives continued to look around the apartment, keeping an eye out for anything else that might look out of place but found nothing. As the forensics team continued to process the scene, Paul and Bryce left them to their work, departing the apartment and stepping out into the hallway.

"Let's start questioning the neighbours and taking statements." Paul said, "I'll take Cruickshank and see if he's our man. The downstairs tenants aren't home. You take the people on the next floor up."

"Why don't we interview Cruickshank together?" Bryce scowled.

"You wanna be here all day? The sooner we get everyone interviewed, the sooner we can get back to the office and start putting everything together."

Paul hoped that sounded plausible. In reality, he wanted to keep Bryce away from Cruickshank for the moment. He wanted the initial interview to be calm and non-confrontational. Bryce, in his current mood, was likely to be more combative. That was unlikely to be very helpful at this point. They can play 'good cop bad cop' later if they need to.

Bryce grunted in his usual inarticulate style but didn't object further. He turned on his heel and proceeded up the stairs. Paul let out a breath he didn't realise he had been holding on to and straightened his tie. Bryce must have missed lunch today. His partner was always extra cranky when he skipped meals.

Paul had also listened to the odd Triple Zero phone recording Bryce had mentioned, and wasn't sure what to expect from Mr. Cruickshank. His voice had been soft yet masculine, and Paul got the impression Cruickshank was a few years younger than himself. His demeanour on the phone was calm, bordering on clinical, but with a strange evenness. An unusual reaction for someone who had just discovered his neighbor, and presumably friend, brutally murdered. But shock can do funny things to people. That's why Paul felt it was important to keep an open mind for the time being.

He dismissed the uniformed officer standing guard outside Cruickshank's apartment, cleared his throat, then knocked on the apartment door.

Chapter 3

JAROD HAD RETURNED to his work on the Hungarian translation after the police officer in the hallway had asked him to remain in his apartment. He didn't see any harm in finishing his project while he waited for the Homicide detectives to interview him.

Unperturbed by the hive of activity across the hall, Jarod concentrated on the task at hand. Once the translation was polished to his liking, he sent the completed document through to his client via email. A few minutes later, his client sent through an instant money transfer via PayPal and a short email thanking Jarod for his excellent work.

A sharp knock at the front door drew his attention from his laptop, and Jarod moved across the room to answer it. Upon opening the door, Jarod was presented with a tall, strongly built man in his early forties. He had a sharp, angular jaw with a dusting of dark stubble and piercing green eyes that were bright like emeralds. His thick, dark hair was cut short and neat, and Jarod detected the slightest hint of spicy, masculine cologne. The man looked tired, his face was drawn with fatigue. His wrinkled shirt and poorly knotted tie suggested someone who had been running late for work. He produced a badge from his pocket and presented it to Jarod.

"Detective Paul Kincaid, Melbourne City Homicide. May I come in, Mr. Cruickshank?"

"Certainly," Jarod replied, stepping aside and allowing the detective entry. "I was about to make myself a cup of tea. Can I offer you something to drink?"

"Thank you. Coffee, if you have it. White with two, please." Kincaid replied absently, looking around the room, his eyes racking over every object, taking in every detail. Jarod could see the man, despite his fatigued appearance, had a sharp mind and was clearly assessing everything around him for future reference.

"I'm lactose intolerant. Dairy gives me explosive diarrhoea. I only have soy milk." Jarod said matter-of-factly as he entered the kitchen, switched on the electric kettle, and began organising the coffee mugs.

Kincaid followed in his wake, his expression turning to what appeared to be a grimace, "I'll take it black, thanks." he murmured.

Jarod shrugged and busied himself making a suitably strong cup of instant coffee for the detective, and a lemon herbal tea for himself. It was then he noticed the detective was standing very close, silently watching him like a hawk.

"Sit on the sofa," Jarod said stiffly.

"I'm fine right here, Mr. Cruickshank."

"Haven't you ever seen someone make coffee before?"

"Many times." the corners of the detective's lips rose slightly, in what Jarod thought was a smirk.

"Then why are you watching me now?"

"Well, just making sure you aren't poisoning my coffee." the detective's smirk grew into a grin.

"What makes you think I haven't already poisoned it?"

The detective's grin vanished. Jarod wasn't sure why he said that. There was something about the detective's proximity that was scattering his brain.

Did I just threaten to murder a police officer? What's wrong with me?

"I meant to say, *why* would I poison your coffee?" Jarod tried to backtrack.

"Well, so far, you're top of the list of suspects in the murder of your neighbour," Kincaid said bluntly.

Jarod considered this for a moment as he poured the boiling water into the two waiting cups.

"I suppose that makes some sense. I *did* find Clarissa. I was her neighbour. Depending on her time of death, I may or may not have an alibi. I guess I can't really blame you for thinking I might be a potential murderer."

Kincaid looked at him with an expression he couldn't identify. Jarod had difficulty knowing if he had said something wrong. But usually, when people suddenly went quiet, that was a sign of offense. That being said, the detective's theory was beyond asinine.

"Are you really a detective?"

"Of course!" he said sharply, "Why would you ask that?"

"Well, you think I may be the murderer, yet you seem to think the best way for me to get away with it would be for me to draw attention to myself by blatantly murdering the person sent to investigate me? Let's just say, Sherlock Holmes probably doesn't have to worry about you unseating him as the master detective."

Jarod offered the steaming cup of coffee to Kincaid, but the detective did not attempt to take it. He remained rigidly silent.

"Oh, right. The poison. Here..." Jarod took a quick sip of the coffee to assure the detective his drink wasn't lethal, then offered it again. The detective burst out laughing.

"Are you serious with this?"

"I'm sorry, I don't understand. Why don't we go through to the living room and take a seat?"

Without waiting for a response, Jarod brought the mugs out to the living room, placed them on the coffee table, then took his place in his usual chair, inviting the detective to take a seat on the sofa.

"Sit."

The detective grumbled, but finally took his place on the sofa and took hold of his mug.

"Thank you," Kincaid said softly, then took a tentative sip of the coffee. Jarod had accurately predicted that the detective would prefer his coffee strong, judging by his guest's immediate taking of a larger sip, and his mood perking up. At least he *thought* Kincaid looked more perked up. Jarod still had difficulty reading people's moods. At the very least, the detective seemed to trust that Jarod wasn't trying to poison him. He figured that was probably a good thing.

"I'll start by taking down your personal information." The detective pulled out a small notebook and pen from his pocket.

At the detective's request, Jarod recited his full name, date of birth, address, and phone number.

"Do you have a work number?"

"No, I work from home."

"Doing what?"

"I'm a freelance text translator. I used to be a lecturer in Linguistics and Written Languages at the Melbourne City University. These days, I spend my time translating foreign language books, texts, documents, and other written items."

"Interesting," The detective said absently, continuing to make notes, "Mr. Cruickshank, can you please tell me, in your own words, how you came to discover your neighbour's body?"

Jarod explained about having a key to Clarissa's apartment, about how she had failed to come over that morning, and that he wanted to check that his neighbour was alright.

"So you have free access to her apartment?" the detective asked as he took notes in a small notebook.

"Well, she gave me a key in case of emergencies. I've rarely had cause to use it. I knew she wanted the book urgently for her grandson, so I figured she wouldn't mind me coming over to drop it off."

"Book?"

"Yes, a book on Ancient Egypt. Clarissa's grandson needed it to do a project at school. It took a while to dig out of my collection. Clarissa was supposed to pick it up this morning before heading out for the day, but she never showed up. When I realised, I decided to drop the book over to her, and check to make sure she was well."

Kincaid nodded. He continued to make notes. Jarod picked up his mug of tea and absently sipped at it.

"I'd like to go over your movements for the last day or so. Starting from when you woke up yesterday."

"Yesterday, I was at home all day. My assistant, Troy was here for part of the day, but he left for classes after lunch. I finished working around five pm. I washed up, then walked to the Imperial Dragon down the road, where I had dinner. I walked home and got back at around seven-thirty. I spent the evening reading and went to bed at around eleven"

"And today?"

"I didn't leave the apartment until I went across the hall with the book. That was at about one o'clock. I've been here ever since the first police officers arrived."

Kincaid's brow was furrowed, concentrating on taking down his statement. Jarod also suspected the detective was frustrated.

"When you entered Mrs. Wainwright's apartment, you found her on the floor. Did you attempt to render assistance? CPR?"

"No."

Kincaid's eyebrows suddenly lifted, "You didn't try to render aid? Why not?"

"Her throat had been slashed open and most of her blood was on the walls and floor. What aid could I possibly have offered?" Jarod replied cooly.

"You didn't check for a pulse?"

"No."

"You didn't check if she was breathing?"

"I could see her windpipe, Detective. Her skin was pale and blue. It was a fair assumption that her injuries were non-survivable and well beyond my abilities to reverse." Jarod sipped his tea again. Kincaid's expression was unreadable.

"Forgive me, but you don't seem to be particularly phased by any of this. I understand the two of you were friends?"

"Yes, we knew each other for several years."

"Yet, you act like you don't care that your friend is dead."

Here we go...

Jarod put down his tea, "Well, I don't really. But it's not out of maliciousness. I'm just not physically capable."

"Not capable?"

Jarod straightened his shoulders and prepared to deliver the speech he had given seemingly hundreds of times before.

"I have an acquired brain injury. I was in a car accident a few years ago and I suffered neurological damage. As a result, I don't really feel emotions anymore. I also have difficulty reading people's facial expressions, so it makes it hard for me to judge how others are feeling. So, if I seem unfeeling or if what I'm saying is inappropriate, it's because I have difficulty reading the room, so to speak. I apologise. It's beyond my control."

"I see," Kincaid said, nodding, and he continued to make notes. Jarod wasn't sure how to interpret the detective's current expression. He guessed he was confused, or possibly skeptical? Jarod couldn't be certain.

"So you can't feel anything at all? That sounds horrible," the detective stared at Jarod with those penetrating green eyes. Jarod wasn't sure what that facial expression meant. Perhaps he thought Jarod was lying.

"It has its ups and downs. But for the most part, I find it gives me an objectivity others often lack. If you like, I can give you the phone number of my neurologist if you need to verify my condition."

"Thank you. I'll also take your assistant's details. I'll need to speak to him too." Kincaid scribbled down the details as Jarod recited the requested information. He then closed the notepad and returned it to his pocket.

"Well, Mr. Cruickshank. I'll need to verify your alibi, but no doubt I'll have more questions for you soon. Thank you for your time." Kincaid stood, shook Jarod's hand, then headed for the front door. Jarod's hand tingled from the brief contact. It was warm and electric. He wasn't sure what that was about.

"You're welcome. Oh, Detective? Before you go..."

Kincaid stopped and turned around.

"My book on Ancient Egypt? Would it be possible to get it back?"

"Why? Is it important?"

"I'd like to ensure Clarissa's grandson gets it so he can use it for his project."

"You're worried about that, huh?" The detective looked confused by Jarod's explanation.

"I made a commitment to him, and I honour my commitments, Detective. The boy has already lost his grandmother. I don't want him to screw up his school project too."

The detective's expression changed. It seemed to soften. Jarod hoped that was a good sign. He'd really like to ensure Riley got the book as soon as possible.

"It's been taken into evidence. But since the book was brought to the crime scene by you after the fact, I should be able to get it cleared quickly and returned to you. I'll be in touch."

"Thank you."

Kincaid smiled, nodded his goodbye, then departed, leaving Jarod alone again.

~

Later that afternoon, Jarod found himself at a loose end. He had no further work to do, so he decided to call his sister. Jarod tried to call Caroline at least once a week to keep in contact. Although he didn't always see eye to eye with his sibling, especially after the accident and the incessant mothering she inflicted upon him in its wake, he tried to maintain a good relationship with her. Since their parents had retired and moved to Canada several years ago, Caroline was the only family Jarod had left in Australia these days.

"Hello?" Caroline answered after the fourth ring.

"Caroline, how are you?"

"Jarod? I'm good. What's happening?"

"Not much. Well, Clarissa is dead."

"Oh no! She was such a lovely old lady. Was it her heart?"

"No, she was murdered."

There was a sharp silence on the line. For the second time that day, Jarod thought his call had been disconnected.

"Did... did you say she was murdered?"

"Yes. I found her this afternoon in her apartment. I've just finished speaking with a police detective."

"Oh my God, Jarod!" Caroline shrieked.

"Calm down, Caroline. It's all being sorted out."

"Sorted out? Are you kidding me? Your neighbour is murdered and you say it's being 'sorted out'?"

Jarod couldn't understand his sister's reaction. It's not like he was the one who got murdered. Caroline only met Clarissa briefly after the accident.

"You have to move home, Jarod. Right now!"

"But, I am home."

"No, home to Sydney with me. It's not safe for you down there. You can't be serious about staying in such a dangerous neighbourhood." Caroline was almost screaming.

"Dangerous neighbourhood? I think you're overreacting a little bit. I mean, to be fair, this is the first murder in the neighbourhood, to my knowledge. Aren't you jumping the gun a little?"

"Jumping the gun? No! And the fact you can't recognise how bad this is just reinforces what I've been saying all along. You can't live on your own anymore. You can't look after yourself properly."

"I'm not on my own. I have my clients. I have Troy. I have Clarissa. Well, I don't have Clarissa any more, I guess. But you know what I mean. I'm perfectly fine down here in Melbourne."

"You need someone to look after you. Please, please come home. Jarod, I'm worried about you."

"Goodness, Caroline, stop carrying on. You almost sound like Mum."

Another deathly silence came over the phone line. Jarod wondered if there was something wrong with his phone.

"Did you seriously just say that? How dare you!" Caroline seethed.

"I'm sorry, sis. I didn't mean to offend you. But, I really don't need anyone to look after me. I'm doing just fine on my own. I don't need you trying to control my life. I'm not an invalid."

"Yes, you are! You have a serious brain injury, for God's sake, Jarod! Clearly, your judgement is impaired, otherwise, you would realise I'm just trying to help you."

Jarod couldn't tell, but he suspected that his sister was upset with him. Either that, or she was angry at him for calling. Perhaps he should have asked if this was a good time to chat?

"Look, I have to go. I'm okay and I'm not in danger. I'm fine here in Melbourne and I certainly don't need to move back to Sydney. Take care, Caroline. I'll talk to you later."

Jarod ended the call before his sister could resume her shrieking. Caroline was always over emotional and quick to panic. Perhaps calling her with the news of Clarissa's death had been a mistake. He had just been trying to keep his sister up to date on the latest happenings in his life. It was times like this, Jarod wished he was still capable of being a bit more subtle with his conversation skills. Or at the very least, better at reading people's reactions. Telephone calls were a nightmare because any physical cues were cut off. Not that he was that good at reading body language anymore.

Jarod returned to his laptop. No new emails and no new work requests. He shut down the computer, figuring he had earned an early mark from work. He went to one of the bookshelves that lined the room, selected a book, and got comfortable in his chair. He opened the book and began to read, allowing the rest of the world to melt away as he lost himself in the symphony of words on the page.

Chapter 4

PAUL AND BRYCE spent the rest of the day speaking to the victim's family, hoping they could establish a possible motive for Clarissa Wainwright's murder. However, the victim's daughter, Wainwright's only living relative besides her young grandson, was as equally baffled by her mother's brutal death. On the face of things, the old woman had seemed to live a quiet, law-abiding life and didn't have any enemies to speak of.

By six pm, they had run out of relevant people to question or promising leads to pursue. The two detectives returned to the station to begin the monumental task of combing through all the evidence gathered thus far, along with all the witness statements. For the moment, all they could really do was verify alibis, at least until the medical examiner and forensic reports came in.

Bryce was still convinced Jarod Cruickshank was their prime suspect, but after what was probably one of the strangest interviews he had ever conducted, Paul wasn't so certain. Sure, the guy was very strange, with his odd behaviour and cool, emotionless speech. He could easily be misconstrued as menacing or even ominous. But acting in an unusual manner was far from unequivocal proof of guilt.

Paul also couldn't help being distracted by how the odd little man made him feel on a personal level. He had to admit, Jarod's slim build; his quiet voice balanced with the way he openly spoke his mind; the fact that he was in his mid-thirties but looked like he was in his mid-twenties; those cute, nerdy glasses. Not to mention his total lack of over-emotional drama put Jarod in stark contrast to the brash, loud, needy, and emotionally erratic nature of his ex. But more than anything, Paul liked the fact that, in the face of everything, Jarod had been concerned about getting that Egyptian book to the victim's grandson. For someone who claimed not to feel anything, Paul couldn't help but feel that Jarod was displaying just a little emotion in that simple act of kindness. He also found it hard to picture Justin doing the same thing under the same circumstances.

In another time and place, Paul would have been seriously tempted to ask Jarod out on a date. To take him out on the town and sweep him off his feet. But given Paul's track record in the romance department, not to mention the fact that Jarod was currently a murder suspect, Paul decided it was best if he tried to suppress his inappropriate feelings and concentrate on his work.

But damn, the sweet little guy was cute...

The two detectives decided to concentrate on confirming or disproving Jarod's alibi should be their priority. If they could disprove Jarod's alibi for the previous evening, it would allow them to focus on him as a viable suspect. Proving his alibi to be true would mean they could rule him out as a suspect and focus their investigation elsewhere.

"The M.E. on the scene estimated the victim's time of death to be around six-thirty pm. According to his statement, Cruickshank claimed to be at the Imperial Dragon Chinese Restaurant at that time. If we can confirm his alibi, that will rule him out as a suspect." Paul surmised.

"I still reckon he's the perp," Bryce grumbled, "But I guess I could head over to the Imperial Dragon now and ask if any of the staff saw him. They might even have security camera footage too." he said, suddenly excited. Bryce quickly pulled on his jacket and gathered up his keys and phone.

"Bring me back some prawn crackers!" Paul called out to his partner, trying to hold back his laughter, as he watched Bryce practically run across the open-plan office, heading directly toward the lifts. Paul knew full well that the reason Bryce had jumped at the chance to visit the Chinese restaurant had nothing to do with clearing Jarod's alibi, and everything to do with his burly partner being hungry.

Paul focused on accessing the City of Melbourne CCTV network. Unlike other cities, Melbourne's public security camera network was still in its infancy. Only some of the streets and public areas in Northcote were covered at this point. Paul could only hope that the route Jarod said he used to walk to and from the restaurant was monitored by the network.

After an hour or so, Paul had managed to gain access to the relevant footage. Unfortunately, only part of Jarod's route was covered by cameras, but hopefully, the footage they had would be enough to prove or disprove his alibi.

Paul scanned through the footage from about a block away from Jarod's building and quickly located him walking down the street in the direction of the restaurant. He then used the footage to follow Jarod's journey in real-time, watching closely until Jarod reached a small park that was not covered by the public cameras. However, the footage thankfully resumed on the other side of the park and was mostly complete until Jarod reached the Imperial Dragon exactly when Jarod said he did. His return journey on foot also lined up with Jarod's statement precisely. If Bryce could confirm Jarod didn't leave the restaurant during his meal, his alibi was confirmed and Jarod would be in the clear.

Moments later, the open-plan office, which was all but deserted compared to during the day shift, was suddenly swamped by the unmistakable aroma of Chinese food. Bryce returned with two bags crammed full of take away containers.

"Tell me that's not all for you!"

Bryce muttered under his breath for a moment, as if weighing up some great decision, then reluctantly handed one of the bags over to Paul.

"Thanks, mate. I was starting to get hungry. How did it go at the restaurant?"

"The weirdo's in the clear," Bryce said through a mouthful of Special Fried Rice, "The owner confirmed Cruickshank's alibi, and they even showed me the camera footage from inside the restaurant. He never left the table for a moment during his meal."

Paul was elated and couldn't help but break out into a face-splitting smile. He knew Jarod wasn't a murderer.

"I don't know why you look so happy. We're back to square one. I was sure the little weirdo was our guy." Bryce moaned as he looked at the stacks of paperwork they had to review that currently covered his desk.

"You might want to drop the 'weirdo' stuff, mate. The poor guy has a brain injury. He can't help his behaviour."

"Oh no. Please tell me you don't have the hots for him!" Bryce said a little too loudly.

"Will you keep your voice down?" Paul quietly growled.

"Everyone knows your gay, mate. It's hardly a secret!"

"That doesn't mean I want everyone in the station knowing my business," Paul muttered between his clenched teeth.

"You do! You think he's a little hotty! Oh my God. You really do have bad taste in men!" Bryce guffawed.

"Shut up, Bryce! You're single too!"

"Yeah, by choice. I'm happy playing the field. I'm certainly not looking for Mrs. Right."

Paul was getting frustrated. He liked Bryce. He was a good partner and a close mate, but sometimes he could be a real pain in the arse. The last thing he wanted was to be having a loud, in-depth discussion about his love life in the middle of the office.

"Can we please focus on the matter at hand? Since our prime suspect is out, we need to look at everything we've gathered so far. See if we can find something that might lead us to our killer. Or at least, uncover a possible motive."

Bryce cleared his food to one side of his desk and started going through the witness statements and crime scene photos, pausing to take bites of his Peking Duck now and again.

Paul focused on the photographs of the bloody symbols the killer drew on the wall. He used Google on his laptop to bring up images of various symbols and alphabets, hoping he would somehow find something comparable. But without knowing exactly what he was looking for, he wasn't going to get very far. The police had language experts on staff, so Paul emailed the relevant photos through to them, marked priority, and hoped that someone would recognise the symbols.

He also considered the possibility that the symbols were not a language at all, but some kind of code. The police had coding experts too, so he emailed them as well. Beyond that, there wasn't much more he could do this evening. He had been exhausted all day, and somehow managed to struggle through his fatigue. But now he was done. He packed everything up, told Bryce he was calling it a night, and would return the tomorrow, hopefully with a fresh pair of eyes and some fresh ideas. This case desperately needed them.

Chapter 5

JAROD WOKE UP early the next morning after tossing and turning for most of the night. His dreams had been a strange mixture of disjointed images. Clarissa dead in her apartment; the bloody, hand-drawn symbols on the wall; Detective Kincaid smiling at him; and a dark, ominous figure lurking in the shadows.

When he went to check if he had any text messages, Jarod noticed his phone was switched off. He had forgotten that he had powered off the device after his call with Caroline, as Jarod wanted some peace and quiet after a long and eventful day. Switching the phone back on, there was a flood of messages from both his sister and Troy.

Troy Merrick, his part-time personal assistant, and housekeeper was a young, free-spirited university student who had been working for Jarod for just over a year. Troy took care of most of the household duties like laundry, light cleaning, and keeping the kitchen cupboards stocked with the essentials. For his translation business, Troy handled all the invoicing, accounts, and maintained his website.

Despite being sassy, outspoken, and highly critical of Jarod's fashion choices, the fair-haired twink with bright blue eyes and what many described as a 'cheeky smile' had a heart of gold and a strong work ethic. Best of all, Troy was not one to take offense easily. If Jarod ever accidentally slipped up and said something inappropriate, Troy's immediate response would be to say something even more inappropriate in return – usually accompanied by some exaggerated finger snapping. Jarod would be lost without Troy and considered him not only a valued colleague but the closest thing he had to a friend.

The text messages from Troy were mostly requests for information regarding Clarissa's death, and enquiries into Jarod's welfare. He quickly replied that he was fine and that he would speak to him when Troy arrived for work in a few hours.

The messages from his sister were increasingly hysterical demands that Jarod start thinking about his health and safety, and for him to return to Sydney. Jarod immediately deleted them without a reply. He had already said everything he needed to say on the matter. He didn't understand why his sister required him to repeat himself over and over.

Jarod was just finishing up breakfast and reading the morning news on his iPad when he heard the lock on the front door click. The door swung open and in burst his assistant, dressed in tight, sparkling gold hot pants and a skimpy, painfully neon pink tank top that bore the words '*Naughty Boi*' in large black letters.

"Morning Boss! How do I look?"

"Hideous," Jarod commented without looking up from his iPad.

"You didn't even look!" Troy whined.

Jarod looked.

"Hideous. Why are you dressed like that?"

"I just came from my workout."

"Where was your workout? 80's Night at The Peel?"

"The Peel? Pfft! You are sooo 2009. You need to update your Melbourne Gay references almost as much as you need to update your phone."

"My phone is perfectly serviceable, thank you."

"It's a Nokia 6610. That brick doesn't even have a touchscreen!" Troy discarded his satchel bag and walked into the kitchen to grab a bottle of chilled water, as he always did before he started work.

"So..." Troy sat down at the table next to Jarod and immediately moved the iPad out of reach, "Wanna tell me all about yesterday?"

Jarod had to think for a moment, unsure what Troy was referring to.

"Um, I completed the Hungarian translation. The payment came through. You'll find everything on the email account."

"And?" Troy said, looking slightly impatient.

"I'm almost out of instant coffee. Add it to the shopping list." Jarod tried to reach for the iPad, but Troy slapped his hand away. Jarod wasn't sure what was going on, but he didn't like it.

"Seriously? We aren't going to talk about your neighbour getting sliced and diced?"

"Oh, that."

"Yes! That! Oh my God, Jarod! What the hell happened?"

"Clarissa died. I found her. I called the police. They came and interviewed me. There isn't much to tell, really."

"Not much to tell?! Are you kidding me with this?"

"How did you know what happened to Clarissa?"

"Duh! It was all over the news last night. Everyone's calling it the Northcote Axe Massacre. Plus I had some giant, hairy bear of a police detective show up at my place last night. He questioned me for ages about you. Seemed to think you're the axe murderer."

"Don't be so ridiculous. Clarissa wasn't killed with an axe. She was stabbed to death with a kitchen knife." Jarod said mildly as he gathered his breakfast plates and took them to the kitchen.

"Oh my God! So, you actually *saw* her? Holy crap, that's messed up. Are you okay?"

"Why wouldn't I be? Now, if you don't mind, I had plenty of murder and intrigue yesterday. I would prefer it if we could just get back to our normal routine today."

Troy was momentarily silent as if considering his words. He took a deep breath and slowly let it out.

"Okay, whatever you need," he said in a soft, calm voice, "I'm so sorry for your loss. If there's anything I can do, you just let me know." Troy then came over and wrapped Jarod in a tight hug, which Jarod was not expecting.

"Um, thank you. I promise I'm fine. I just want to focus on my work."

"No worries. I'll check the overnight emails and set you up with any new jobs. Then I'll get on with the household stuff."

Troy set himself up on the couch, pulled his laptop out of his bag, and began typing away furiously. Jarod went to his desk, opened his laptop, and began his workday.

The morning went smoothly and quickly. Jarod finished a couple of quick document translations while Troy updated the accounts and organised the invoicing. Once he had finished tidying the apartment at around lunchtime, Troy gathering his belongings, bid his farewell, and departed for his afternoon lectures at the university.

With Troy gone, Jarod was at a loose end. He had no further work to complete. The apartment was tidy and he didn't need to grocery shopping since Troy had already been out to grab a few items earlier. With nothing else to do, he headed for the kitchen and made himself a cup of Camomile tea.

He decided a half-day off work would be good after recent events. He perused the bookshelves, looking for something to immerse himself in. Proust, perhaps. Or maybe one of the Russian epics. Something he could really get his teeth into.

Jarod finally settled on Anna Karenina (in the original Russian, of course) and had just begun reading the first line, when he was suddenly interrupted by a sharp, insistent knocking on his front door. Jarod put down the book and answered the door.

"You did it, didn't you? You actually did it, didn't you!"

Justin Porter, Jarod's ex-boyfriend from several years ago was standing at his door looking flustered. His face was red and he seemed to be brimming with nervous energy, judging by the way he was bouncing on the balls of his feet.

Jarod hadn't seen or heard from Justin since their breakup. Well, 'breakup' implies their separation was mutual. Justin dumped Jarod unceremoniously while Jarod lay in the ICU. They had met only a few weeks before the accident, and Justin decided that *he* simply couldn't deal with being in a relationship with a 'brain-damaged cripple', as he so charmingly put it. The fact that Justin chose to do this while Jarod lay in a hospital bed, recovering from emergency surgery and unable to speak, was neither here nor there.

Jarod wasn't worried about the termination of their relationship. He had barely known the man as it was, and Justin appeared to only be interested in Jarod because 'geeks' were 'in' at the time. Since then, the two men had never spoken or even texted each other.

"I saw the news report online this morning and I knew immediately it was you."

"Hello Justin, it's nice to see you again after all this time. May I offer you a beverage?" Jarod said mildly, hoping the offering of refreshment might calm his ex down a little.

"Tea with a murdering bastard? No thanks!" Justin spat out.

"Would you prefer coffee?" Jarod offered, hoping this would please his guest more.

"Why? Why would you do it? I mean, I know the accident turned you into a psycho, but I certainly never expected you would do anything like this. Clarissa was a sweet old lady who never hurt a fly. How could you take to her with an axe?" Justin had tears streaming down his face.

"I didn't kill Clarissa, Justin. I found her and reported her death to the police. If I killed her, why would I do that?"

"Because you're a psycho. I'm going to make sure you get what you deserve. I'm calling the police!" Justin proclaimed loudly.

"The police are already here," A booming voice replied from the front door. Jarod and Justin turned as one and saw the imposing figure of Detective Paul Kincaid, his face looking hard as stone.

"Justin, what the hell are you doing here?" he said in an even yet slightly rumbling tone. Jarod found it made his stomach feel funny like it was suddenly filled with butterflies.

That's so weird. What's that about?

"What am I doing here?" Justin screeched, "What are you doing here?"

"I'm a homicide detective. There was a homicide next door. What do you think I'm doing here?"

Jarod had forgotten his manners. He had one guest without a drink and another waiting to be invited in.

"Please come in, Detective. Justin Porter, this is Detective Paul Kincaid. Detective Kincaid, this is..."

"We've met." Justin said cooly, his gaze never straying from Paul, "Are you here to arrest this psycho? You damned well should be. He killed that poor old lady!"

"No, he didn't. That's why I'm here. Jarod has an airtight alibi. He is no longer a suspect."

"Well, that's good to know," Jarod said, not really knowing what else to say in these circumstances. He'd never been suspected of murder before.

"I don't believe it for a second. I'm telling you, he did it. Just look in his eyes. There's nothing there. He's cold and dead inside. If he didn't kill her, he'll kill *someone* soon. Mark my words!" Justin huffed with righteous indignation and headed for the door.

Jarod blocked Justin's exit and moved in close to him, looking him straight in the eye.

"If you think I'm a killer," he said mildly, "Do you really think bursting in here and making loud accusations was a smart thing to do? Do you really think that's a winning formula for your long term survival?" Jarod gave his ex a slow, wide smile in that way Troy always said looked unintentionally creepy.

Justin paled, his eyes big as saucers.

"Did you hear that? He threatened to kill me! What more proof do you need? Arrest him!"

Paul's expression was more unreadable than usual, "I didn't hear a specific threat, Mr. Porter. Now, I think you should be on your way. Mr. Cruickshank and I have some business to discuss."

Justin's face went bright red again, then he fled the apartment, not bothering to close the door behind him.

"And people think I don't have a sense of humour..." Jarod muttered to himself. Paul burst out laughing.

"That was a cruel trick to play on him, but to be honest, I couldn't think of anyone more deserving. What was he doing here anyway, besides accusing you of murder?"

"Oh, Justin is my ex-boyfriend from a few years ago."

"Yeah, Melbourne is a small city..." Paul laughed again and clarified the observation by stating that he had dated Justin in the past.

"Well, it's nice to know I'm not the only one with lousy taste in men," Jarod said but noticed the smile instantly vanished from the detective's face.

"Oh, that was probably one of those things I shouldn't say out loud. Sorry, I didn't mean to be offensive. I have trouble..."

"It's okay. No need to explain. I understand. Look the reason I came around, besides letting you know that you are no longer a suspect, was to ask for your help."

"I see. Sit down. What do you need?" Jarod directed the detective to the couch as he closed the front door.

"Did you notice the message written on the wall in Mrs. Wainwright's apartment?"

"I did, but I was more focused on her body and summoning emergency services."

"Would you mind taking a look at a photo of the message?"

"Certainly."

Paul pulled out his phone, opened the photos app, and found the appropriate image. He handed the device to Jarod and he examined the bloody symbols carefully.

"I sent this image to all of our language experts, but so far, no one has been able to translate them."

Jarod continued to look at the symbols. They looked vaguely familiar, like something he had seen a long time ago.

"Looks like crudely formed Cuneiform characters. Possibly Linear A or one of the older Elamite tongues..." Jarod muttered absently.

"You... you actually recognise this writing?"

"I studied several ancient languages when I was at university. These characters were used several thousand years ago by multiple civilisations across the Ancient Middle East."

"Can you translate it?"

"I'm not sure. It's not something I get much call for in my work these days. I'll have to refer to my notes. Assist me."

With that, Jarod stood and walked into the library room, Paul chasing after him.

"What do you need me to do?" The detective asked, sounding a little confused, Jarod surmised.

"That bookshelf next to you. Go through the notebooks and pull out any labeled 'Cuneiform' or 'Ancient Languages'. It could be marked 'Babylon' or 'Mesopotamia' too. Grab anything along those lines. I haven't used these notes for years and haven't got around to properly ordering and cataloging them yet."

Paul began going through the shelves while Jarod went through another. He found a couple of old textbooks on Cuneiform language forms from his university days and put them aside.

Within minutes, the two men had a large cardboard box filled with books and handwritten notes. The box was heavy, but Paul's muscular arms didn't seem to protest the weight. That funny feeling in Jarod's stomach returned.

Maybe there was something wrong with the tea?

"If you just place those down on my desk, I can begin working immediately."

"Actually, would you mind coming down to the station to work on the translation? I'd like to keep any knowledge of the message out of the public eye. Or the media for that matter. If you work from there, I can keep the information under wraps more easily."

Jarod considered this for a moment. Working from the police station would be an awkward change of environment. He preferred to work in the relative peace and quiet of his home. But Jarod also recognised the importance of this translation, and that some compromises would need to be made.

"Will I have a quiet place to work? I'll also need internet access, a whiteboard, some..."

"I promise, I can arrange anything you need. I can't guarantee the office will be super quiet, but I can set you up in one of the conference rooms. It should keep the noise of the main office down to a dull roar." Paul smiled. Jarod assumed that was a joke of some kind.

Were police stations really that loud? Only one way to find out, I guess.

"Lead the way, Detective."

Chapter 6

WHEN PAUL DECIDED to visit Jarod that day, it had been little more than a thinly veiled excuse to see the cute little man one more time. There was no police procedure that required him to inform a person of interest that their alibi had been confirmed, or to relay that they were no longer considered a suspect.

His excuse for asking Jarod to assist with the translation of the symbols had been equally thin. He hadn't seriously expected Jarod to be able to help since none of the police experts had been able to make anything of the morbid message. However, it was clear that Paul had significantly underestimated Jarod's skills as a linguist.

Just standing in the open doorway of Jarod's apartment, quietly observing as the strange little man was being berated by Justin made the trip worthwhile. It gave him the opportunity to study Jarod closely. While Justin screeched and screamed, Jarod merely stood there, totally unfazed by his ex's exasperating behaviour. Jarod just stared at him calmly and serenely through his round, wire-rimmed glasses.

Paul raked his gaze over the smaller man. Like during their first encounter, Jarod's soft, slightly tousled, light brown hair could almost be described as "artfully messy," but only if his hair had been styled that way on purpose. Paul knew instantly it was not. As for Jarod's attire, it aged him prematurely. His clothes were the kind of thing you would expect someone twice his age to wear, combining functionality with efficiency, with no consideration for modern style or the latest fashion trends. The outfit covered a short yet slender form, tapering down to a pair of narrow hips and slight, gangly legs. Paul idly wondered what it would be like to feel those legs wrapped around his waist as he...

Paul snapped out of it and realised standing there ogling a person of interest in his case was probably not the smartest of ideas and had chosen that moment to announce his presence to the two men.

So without having intended it, Paul found now himself in his car with Jarod and a large cardboard box filled with old books, skimming through the midday traffic toward the police station.

Bryce is going to have a field day with this.

Paul hadn't informed his partner about the plan to bring Jarod in to assist with the translation, mainly because the whole plan had come about on the spur of the moment, and his partner's reaction was unlikely to be positive.

Jarod sitting next to him, his close proximity in the confines of the car, was making it difficult for Paul to keep focused on the job. He had a case to solve. A killer to catch. But Paul could also smell Jarod's aftershave. It's mild, lightly floral scent was somehow amplified in the close quarters. It almost reminded him of a spring breeze. It was intoxicating, and Paul could feel his trousers becoming tighter and slightly uncomfortable.

FOCUS!

"So, how long did you and Justin date?" Paul asked, hoping a little conversation would help to bring his body to heel.

"A few weeks. I'm not even sure I'd call it 'dating' as such. Justin was always trying to drag me to nightclubs and dance parties. I never had much interest in those things. After the accident, Justin stuck around for a little while, but then decided I was too much of a burden for him."

"What a prick," Paul said, shaking his head.

"I wasn't upset. Well, I should say, I wouldn't have been upset if I were capable. It's not like I knew the guy very well."

"I had more or less the same experience, minus the car accident. Justin and I wanted different things in a relationship, and he simply couldn't handle the fact that being cop sometimes meant I would have irregular work hours and social plans would have to be cancelled now and again."

"I would have thought that was obvious. Cops aren't exactly famous for their nine to five schedules. Surely Justin must have realised that from the beginning."

Paul looked over at Jarod. He actually understood his position. Justin never seemed to accept how important Paul's work responsibilities were, but Jarod appeared to without a second's hesitation.

I need to be careful. I could really fall for this one...

Soon, Paul was pulling into the underground carpark beneath the police station, parking in his assigned space and escorting Jarod up to the Homicide offices. The place was packed with people and the workplace noise was reverberating across the open plan area. A stark contrast to the relative quiet of the previous evening. They headed towards Paul and Bryce's desks. Bryce was seated, going through paperwork and grumbling to himself. Jarod quietly took a seat next to Paul's desk while Paul filled his partner in on the latest developments.

"Bryce, I may have found us someone who can translate the symbols," Paul announced, placing the heavy box of books down on his desk.

Bryce almost smiled, but then locked eyes with Jarod. His expression instantly morphed into a scowl that could strip paint.

"You can't be serious!"

"He's a linguist and a translator. Jarod recognises the symbols."

"Does he now? Well, isn't that interesting?" Bryce said snidely.

"We haven't got much to lose. Our experts haven't come up with anything, have they?"

"He's a person of interest, Paul. This is completely irregular."

"We cleared him as a suspect. His alibi checked out. We know he didn't do it!" Paul was quickly losing patience with his partner's one-eyed approach to this case. The two detectives stared each other down.

"I don't like this. But, I know you'll just bitch at me until you get your own way. Be it on your own head."

Paul almost choked on his own tongue. Bryce virtually never backed down from an argument. Either he finally realised he was being ridiculous, or...

He thinks this is going to blow up in my face.

Deciding not to push his luck, Paul grabbed the box of books, intent on getting Jarod set up in a conference room as soon as possible. As he walked away, he realised Jarod wasn't following. He turned around and saw him talking with Bryce.

"Huh?" Bryce snorted.

"I said, did you have breakfast this morning?" Jarod said evenly.

"Why?"

"Well, based on my observations, you have a flushed face; you're growling a lot; your facial expression looks like someone who's concentrating on something. I thought you might have skipped breakfast, hadn't had enough dietary fibre and were therefor constipated." Jarod said mildly as if he were reading out a shopping list.

Paul's heart stopped. If he laughed at that comment, Bryce would kill him stone dead.

"What the actual fuck?!" Bryce roared. Jarod just sat there, completely unmoved by the beast about to tear him to shreds.

Shit!

"Jarod, why don't we get you set up over here. Leave Bryce alone." Paul all but dragged Jarod away from Bryce, who looked about five seconds away from having an aneurism.

He escorted Jarod into a vacant conference room. It was basically a glass box at the end of the office. Paul dumped the heavy box on the large table that dominated the room and started unpacking everything.

"There's a whiteboard in here. There should be some pens in the desk drawers over there. I'll get you the Wi-Fi password for your laptop. Need anything else?"

"Some scrap paper to write on, if you have it. Other than that, I should be fine."

Paul pulled some paper out of one of the photocopiers in the main office area, grabbed a copy of the bloody message photo, then returned to the room. He placed the paper and photo on the table, wrote the password for the Wi-Fi on one of the paper sheets, then watched for a moment as Jarod set up his laptop and arranged his notebooks in some sort of order.

Even when he's just working on a computer, I can't keep my eyes off of him.

"I'll be at my desk if you need me."

Jarod nodded absently, not looking up from his screen as he typed away furiously while glancing at one of the notebooks. Paul decided not to disturb him further, he just smiled and turned away.

As Paul approached his desk, Bryce locked eyes with him and his look was a blaze of fury.

"What the fuck are you doing?"

"I was about to ask you the same thing," Paul responded.

"Me?" Bryce was incredulous.

"Yeah, you. The one guy who might be able to give us our first solid lead on this case, and you're jumping all over him and screaming in his face? What the hell his wrong with you?"

"Did you hear what he said to me?"

Paul tried to hide his smirk, but the memory of Jarod asking his partner if he were constipated was just too funny.

"If you laugh, I will beat you to death!"

"C'mon. It's a little funny."

"Seriously, asking something like that. What's his damage?"

"Pre-frontal cortex mainly."

Bryce grunted, obviously confused.

"As I told you, he has brain damage from a car accident. He can't help the things he says. He also has trouble reading people's facial expressions and moods. So cut him a little slack. He's here in his free time helping us. Stop being a dick to him."

Bryce visibly deflated. Paul knew his partner well. He could get a little carried away sometimes, but if you called him out, he would eventually realise he was out of line.

"Alright. I guess I was being a bit of a dick. So are you two dating or what?"

"What? No! I like him, but no. I don't think that's a good idea."

"Oh yeah, I forgot. You've given up on men and have decided to die alone."

Paul's expression must have been arctic. Bryce froze in place like he was suddenly trapped in a block of ice.

"Shit. Sorry, mate. That was out of line. I didn't..."

"No worries..." Paul said cooly. He returned to his desk and buried himself in paperwork; effectively ending his conversation with Bryce despite the two men literally sitting right next to each other.

Paul was still smarting from that brutal assessment of his love life as he began going through the medical examiner's reports and witness statements again. He let Bryce's harsh words slide over him, like water off a duck's back, because he didn't want to spend an entire day arguing with his partner or giving him the silent treatment. They both had work to do. But the sting of Bryce's blunt words still hurt.

Perhaps his intention to stop dating and just accept life as a lonely single cop was a bit dramatic. God knew he had tried the dating scene and failed miserably every time. Clearly, a new approach was needed. He hadn't met Jarod at a pub or some online dating app.

Perhaps that could make a difference?

However, there was one issue that still hadn't been addressed. Did Jarod even like him? Was Jarod even capable of liking him? Jarod didn't really feel anything. Was Paul Jarod's type? Probably not, given his dating history included Justin. But then again, Paul had dated Justin too. So who knows?

Regardless, any kind of relationship between them would have to wait until the case was over. He was going to be firm on this point above all others. He was already in dangerous territory letting a person of interest get involved in the casework as it was. Adding a romantic component could only be seen as flat-out irresponsible by the top brass.

Paul turned his attention to the M.E.'s report. Clarissa had been stabbed 47 times. No defensive wounds were found. A blunt force trauma was sustained to the back of the head, which would have likely resulted in unconsciousness or even death.

So the killer subdued her by knocking her out, then stabbed her. Interesting...

That explains why no one in the building heard any screams. Clarissa was likely unconscious before she realised what was happening.

No forced entry to the apartment. Clarissa invited the killer in, or the killer had keys. Someone she knew, perhaps?

The murder weapon was a kitchen knife, found at the scene. It was one from a set found in Clarissa's kitchen. The killer didn't bring a stabbing weapon with them.

A murder of opportunity? Or did the killer know he wouldn't need to bring a weapon?

Traces of the victim's blood was found in the bathroom shower drain, suggesting the killer had showered before leaving. That meant they had to have brought a change of clothes with them.

Premeditation. This killing wasn't random. The killer was prepared.

Paul took a moment to look across at the conference room. Through the wall of glass, he could see Jarod stood in front of the whiteboard, concentrating intently at something he was written, his expression neutral.

It was after three pm and Paul hadn't had lunch yet. He would bet good money Jarod hadn't either. He decided they could both use a break. He got up from his desk, stretched lightly, then headed over to the conference room.

"How's it going in here?"

"It's not."

"Having problems?"

"I'm having problems identifying the language structure."

"Well, I'm hungry, and I thought now would be a good time to take a break."

"I prefer to continue working."

"I'm sure, but I think you could use a rest. Come with me and we'll get something to eat. Maybe a break will help you see things with fresh eyes when you get back."

"If you insist."

Paul did insist. Jarod obviously didn't want to admit it, but he clearly had a problem with time management. He'd just sit there and work until he dropped unless someone told him to take a break. No wonder the guy needed to hire a personal assistant.

"We're heading out for some lunch, back soon," Paul said to Bryce as they passed his desk.

"Wait. Jarod!" Bryce called out.

Jarod turned and looked at the hulking cop.

"About before. How I was behaving. I'm sorry. I was completely out of line. Can we start over?" Bryce extended his hand to him.

Jarod moved over to his desk and clasped his hand tightly, shaking it.

"I'll bring you something back for your lunch. Perhaps something with fibre."

And with that, Jarod turned and followed Paul out toward the lifts. Paul may have noticed a slight smile on Bryce's face as the lift doors closed.

Paul had quickly come to realise that, unlike most people, Jarod did not express himself much with his face. He walked around with a fairly neutral expression that, to the unprepared, could almost be mistaken for boredom or disinterest. Justin would probably call it something sassy like 'resting bitch face.'

But as the lift descended to the ground floor, Paul noticed Jarod's expression had subtly shifted. Gone was the neutral blandness, replaced with a slight expression of confusion.

"Is everything okay?" Paul asked.

"It's the symbols. There's something strange about them. It's like... they're familiar to me, but I don't know where from. It's very confusing."

"It's probably something you saw when you were studying at University, but have since forgotten. I'm sure it'll come to you eventually."

"No, it feels like something more than that. I feel like I'm missing something obvious, but I just don't know what."

Chapter 7

THE COFFEE HUT was only a short walk from the police station, so the two men decided against driving. On their short stroll, Paul told Jarod about how he had first been introduced to the cafe by a friend who works in the neighbouring building. Apparently, Paul met this friend, some big wig CEO, during a previous case, and the two of them have been meeting up for lunches and coffee breaks as regularly as their mutual schedules would allow.

Huddled between two looming office buildings, The Coffee Hut was a small but vibrant cafe, typical of the type of establishment Melbourne was famous for. Featuring indoor and outdoor seating, a wide variety of freshly prepared meals and an exotic menu of coffee-based drinks, Jarod was left in no doubt why such a place would be a favourite of his dining companion.

"I hope they do tea, I'm not much of a coffee drinker," Jarod said absently, scanning the menu boards.

"Actually, they have an extensive tea range, plus lactose-free options on the lunch menu."

Jarod was initially impressed that Paul had taken the trouble to remember his dairy issues, but then assumed having a good memory for details probably came hand in hand with being a police detective.

The two men sat at a table in the back corner of the cafe, which was a quieter and more private spot than the rest of the busy establishment. A waitress came over shortly afterwards to take their orders.

Paul ordered a cheeseburger with fries, while Jarod ordered a grilled chicken salad with mango dressing and a cup of mint tea. The waitress quickly darted away to place their orders.

"I'm curious, how did you and Justin Porter meet?" Jarod asked mildly.

"Hookup app. First time I'd ever used one before. Probably the last time too, given how it turned out."

Jarod concluded that with his busy schedule, Paul likely wouldn't have the time to meet men in more traditional settings, so a hookup app wasn't such an unusual option. Jarod had never used one before, but then, he'd never had the need or inclination to seek out a partner. Not since the accident.

"It's strange. I haven't seen or heard from Justin since just after the accident. Then suddenly, years later, he's bursting through my front door and loudly making accusations. Doesn't that seem a little suspicious?"

"I thought it was a little odd too. Extreme, even for Justin. I'll make some discreet inquiries. I don't think he's involved, but it'd be remiss of me to disregard him entirely."

The waitress brought over their drinks, and Paul took a long slurp of his extra-large latte. He made a noise of gratification that triggered the butterflies in Jarod's stomach again.

"Mind if I ask you a personal question?" Paul asked, his eyes squinted slightly as if concentrating.

"Go ahead."

"What's it like? Living without feeling anything?"

"It's difficult to explain. I experience events. I know those events should trigger something. But they don't. I know something is missing, but I don't know what."

"I'm not sure I understand."

Jarod looked around the table for inspiration, and his eyes landed on a small steak knife sitting on his side plate. He picks it up and gestures with it.

"Imagine if I took this knife and stabbed you through the hand with it..."

"This *is* just a hypothetical example, right?" Paul moved back in his chair slightly.

"Of course. It would be inappropriate to stab my dining companion before we've even eaten. I'm not insane." Jarod said blandly.

"That sense of humour of yours is gonna get you in trouble one of these days," Paul said with a wavering chuckle. He settled back in his chair again.

"Anyway, imagine I stab you through your hand. The likely result of this, for you, would be a wound on your hand; bleeding; intense pain; muscular or possibly bone damage. You would be immediately aware of all of these symptoms."

"Yeah, that makes sense," Paul said slowly.

"Now, imagine the same scenario. I stab you through the hand. But you don't notice. You're, let's say, distracted by the conversation we're having. Eventually, you look down and see the knife sticking out of your hand. You know a knife shouldn't be there. You know you should have noticed it penetrating your hand. You know you should be experiencing some sort of sensation. But you aren't. There's nothing there. You're observing the event, but not experiencing it."

Jarod put the knife back down on his side plate, then took a sip of his cooling tea.

"That's what it's like for me. Does that make sense to you?"

After a moment, Paul replies "Yes, it does. I don't know how you live like that, but I think I understand it more, now."

"I live like this because I don't have any other choice. It's who I am."

"Do you ever feel lonely?" Paul asked.

"It's not exactly easy for me to make friends. I wasn't exactly a social butterfly before the accident. There are times where I experience a sense of... isolation, but I'm not sure if that's really loneliness."

"Yeah," Paul said quietly, "I can relate to that. It's not easy meeting people. Sometimes, being alone all the time just sucks."

"Perhaps we can be isolated together," Jarod sipped his tea, "I would welcome your presence anytime you are feeling alone."

Paul smiled at him. He reached across the table, touched Jarod's hand lightly, and it felt like electricity shooting up his arm. The butterflies were back in force and he suddenly felt warm all over.

I wonder if I'm coming down with something?

The waitress returned with their meals, and the two men concentrated on eating rather than talking. Jarod had to agree with Paul's assessment of the cafe. The food was of excellent quality. He would have to tell Troy about this place. His assistant would likely enjoy their extensive coffee menu.

"Do you miss feeling things?" Paul asked.

"I've gotten used to it. My condition allows me to focus on my work without the distractions emotions can bring. But sometimes, I remember what it was like to laugh at someone's joke, or cry at a moving piece of music..."

"When I spoke to your doctor when I was verifying your alibi, he said your brain could rewire itself?"

"It's true, the brain is capable of a remarkable degree of healing and regeneration. Sometimes, it can completely bypass damaged neural pathways and build new synaptic connections. But I've been living with this condition for many years now. While the possibility exists that my condition may improve slightly, it probably would have happened by now if it was ever going to happen."

Paul nodded thoughtfully. Jarod understood the detective's curiosity. There were very few people in the world with his type of acquired brain injury, and the symptoms were atypical enough to provoke the confusion of others.

"Can I bring you guys anything else?" The waitress said as she cleared their lunch plates.

"Yes, I'd like to place an order for take out. Can I have two steak sandwiches? Medium rare. With spicy relish. On whole wheat bread. And can they be toasted? Oh, and a side salad. Light oil dressing. Lot's of green, leafy vegetables. And a large, non-dairy mixed berry smoothie. And can you add some baby spinach to the mix when you make the smoothie? I want to cram in some extra roughage."

The waitress looked momentarily stunned, but quickly recovered and started scribbling down the order. Jarod figured she probably thought he was still hungry.

"It'll be ready in about ten minutes. Is that okay?"

"Perfect. Thank you."

The waitress dashed off to the kitchen and Jarod took another sip of his herbal tea. Paul looked at him with his head tilted slightly.

"What was all that about?"

"Lunch for Bryce. Even if he avoids the salad, I'll get some fibre into him somehow. I have a theory it'll make him feel a lot better."

Paul smiled widely, "Well, I can guarantee you one thing. Whether you were intending too or not, you're about to make a friend for life. Steak sandwiches are his favourite."

~

Upon returning to the police station, Jarod delivered lunch to Bryce at his desk. The giant man abruptly stood up from the stack of paperwork he had been scowling at, shook his hand forcefully, then pulled him into what Paul would later describe as a 'guy clench.' Jarod was treated to a wide, genuine smile from the usually gruff cop, confirming Paul's theory that steak sandwiches would have a beneficial effect on him. Hopefully, the increase in dietary fibre will be equally as beneficial.

Jarod returned to the glass conference room to resume his work on translating the symbols. So far, his translation was not going well. Despite going over his notes on ancient languages, combined with his memories of learning about Cuneiform dialects back at university, he hadn't yet identified what specific language the message was written in.

It was entirely possible that Jarod wasn't reading the symbols correctly. Cuneiform characters are traditionally formed by pressing a specially shaped reed wedge into soft clay. The characters left at Clarissa's house were formed by finger painting. As a result, the symbols were sometimes messy and difficult to differentiate from other, similar Cuneiform characters.

But that wasn't the only problem. Even taking into account the sloppy way the characters were formed, the symbols didn't even make any vague sense. Cuneiform languages all share some basic similarities. But this message features groups of characters put together that don't seem to make any sense in any ancient language Jarod had previously studied. This left Jarod with only three possible explanations:

1) The message is written in a language Jarod is completely unfamiliar with. If this was the case, Jarod would be of no further help. This explanation was, however, highly unlikely, given the message construction and character type should make at least some sense to Jarod. Which it doesn't.

2) It's not written in a language per-se, but some kind of code. If this was the case, without further information about how the code is constructed, or more examples of the code, it would be almost impossible to decipher.

3) The symbols are not a message. They can't be translated because they do not carry a specific linguistic meaning. Their only significance is as part of the killer's ritual or fantasy. In this case, Jarod would be completely out of his depth. They would need a forensic psychologist to glean any hidden meaning or motivation behind the creation of the symbols.

There was something else about the message that was confounding Jarod. The symbols looked familiar. Earlier that day, he had transcribed the bloody message onto the large whiteboard that dominated one end of the conference room. The hope being that, staring at the symbols long enough might trigger some sort of inspiration. So far, Jarod's linguistic muse had failed to appear.

Despite comparing the message to every ancient language form he could think of, nothing seemed to be able to unlock its secrets. Yet, the symbols still looked strangely familiar to Jarod. He couldn't put his finger on why or how. Only that he had a vague sense of having seen something like it before, but the details were obscured from his memory.

Jarod was beginning to feel that same sense of almost frustration he had experienced during the recent Hungarian translation.

"How's it coming?" Paul's voice broke Jarod from his inner musings.

"It's not. I don't understand it. I look at this thing, and I swear I've seen it before. But I can't remember where."

"Well, it's been a long day and I reckon you could use some rest. It's nearly seven pm. I'm going to drive you home, and you can have a fresh start in the morning. That is if you're willing to come back tomorrow?" Paul asked, his eyes laser-focused on Jarod's.

"Of course. I'm committed to assisting in this case in any way I can. I want to find out who killed Clarissa."

~

After driving Jarod back to The Paradiso, Paul insisted on walking him upstairs to his door. Jarod fished out his keys from his messenger bag and began unlocking the door.

"You know, neither of us have had dinner. You could freshen up, and I could take you out somewhere if you like." Paul said softly, sounding almost hesitant. Jarod suspected Paul wanted to spend more time with him but didn't want to outright say he was feeling lonely.

"Well, I am slightly hungry. Very well, I accept your invitation. Come in and sit while I clean myself up."

Jarod put his wallet, keys and phone down on the coffee table, watched as Paul took his usual spot on the couch and told him to help himself to a drink if he was thirsty. Just as Jarod turned to head toward his bedroom, Paul's phone started ringing.

"Kincaid," Paul brusquely answered, "Yeah. About ten minutes away. Alright, I'm on my way."

"Is everything alright?" Jarod asked mildly.

"Duty calls. I have to get back to the station. I'm so sorry, Jarod. I promise to make this up to you."

"Think nothing of it. I have some work to catch up on myself. Will you pick me up in the morning?"

Paul looked momentarily stunned. Jarod played back his last words in his mind, looking to see if anything he had said could be misconstrued as offensive. He didn't think so.

"I'll swing by at eight am," he answered absently, "Are you currently seeing anyone? You know, romantically?" Paul asked, finally breaking the silence.

"No."

"Would you like to go out on a date with me? Not tonight. But another night?"

"Oh, I don't know. I'm not sure that's a good idea. I haven't been on a date in years. I don't really do the whole 'social' thing. Besides, why would you want to date someone like me? I can't feel anything. Surely, you'd want someone who can share and reciprocate your feelings," Jarod was aware he was babbling, though he had no idea why; All that he knew was that he couldn't seem to stop himself, "Plus I'm rude, and easily confused by people, and I don't know if I'm capable of having sex. So, I'm sure that..."

Paul broke off Jarod's babbling by pouncing upon him, pushing him up against the closed bedroom door and pressing close to him, cupping Jarod's face with both hands and enveloping him in a searing kiss. It was rough and possessive, a claiming kiss that had his toes curling and his body shaking. Jarod felt that electrical feeling again, only this time it was all over his body. His skin felt flushed with warmth and his head swam with a giddiness he was unfamiliar with. When Paul broke the kiss, they were both panting desperately for air.

"How was that?" Paul asked with a smile, rubbing his thumb along Jarod's lower lip.

"It was... interesting." Jarod said, still stunned from what had just happened.

"Well, that's a start,' Paul softly chuckled, "Let see what happens from here. I'll pick you up in the morning."

And with that, he lay a soft kiss on Jarod's forehead, opened the apartment door and saw himself out, leaving Jarod feeling slightly flustered. Jarod hadn't felt flustered in years. It was fascinating. It was also a little disturbing.

Chapter 8

THE NEXT DAY, Paul was making his way to Jarod's place through the early morning city traffic. The roads were busy, but Paul wasn't the least bit frustrated at the delay. He was too preoccupied with what had transpired the previous evening.

That kiss.

Just the thought of it had Paul's body vibrating with excitement, even if Jarod's response had been highly subdued. Paul hadn't expected an explosion of emotion from him but was delightfully surprised when Jarod appeared to be, at the very least, thrown off balance by their passionate embrace. Perhaps his hot little nerd with those sweet, kissable lips wasn't quite as emotionless as he had thought? Paul suspected the kiss had been the first intimate activity Jarod had experienced in quite some time, which accounted for how flustered Jarod had appeared afterwards.

Paul knew it was probably a bad idea to involve himself with Jarod in the middle of the case, but the more he got to know him, the more he liked Jarod. When Jarod had started babbling about all the reasons going on a date together was a *bad* idea, something inside Paul just snapped. His resolve crumbled and his restraint was let loose. He was out of control as he dived in to plant his lips upon Jarod's.

He hoped he hadn't made a huge mistake, but the deed was done, and there was nothing to be done about it now. Paul just hoped that he hadn't come off as too aggressive, and scared Jarod away. Not only did he not want to lose the sweet man from his life, but he also needed his help if he was ever to crack the meaning of those damned symbols.

When he arrived at The Paradiso, he parked in a space out the front, walked up the stairs and approached Jarod's door. From within the apartment, he could hear muffled noises. The sound of large, heavy things being moved or dragged around. Paul was instantly on alert.

Is Jarod in danger?

Paul immediately knocked loudly on the door. The noises from within ceased instantly. Moments later, the locks started clicking as they unlocked in turn, and the door swung open to reveal an out of breath Jarod, and another man holding a cardboard box filled with heavy books.

"Is everything alright? I heard noises..."

Jarod shrugged, "Oh, yeah. We were moving some boxes from under my bed out into the living room. Some of them were too heavy for me to move alone, so I got Troy here to come in early and help."

Paul looked over at the other man, a young twink wearing ridiculously short shorts, no shirt, and a backwards, hot pink baseball cap.

"Well, you must be the other detective. I met your friend the other night. I'm Troy, Jarod's assistant," he said as he approached, stalking like a predator eyeing his next meal, offering his hand. Paul accepted it and gave it a powerful squeeze as they shook. Paul smirked ever so slightly when Troy went from a very definite purr to a sharp squeak at the crushing handshake.

Why am I doing this? Am I seriously jealous? Get a grip, Kincaid!

"Troy, heel!" Jarod said distractedly.

Troy harrumphed, but moved away.

"So, why are you rearranging books at this time of the morning?"

"I was thinking about the symbols last night, trying to figure out why they seemed familiar. For some reason, I kept thinking about my childhood, and a book I once had when I was very young. The memory is fuzzy. I looked around, but I couldn't find the book on any of my shelves. Then I remembered I had several old books from my childhood packed up under my bed..."

Jarod started going through the old boxes, picking up various books, examining them, then putting them back. Many of the books were covered in years of dust.

"You think this book might help you with the translation?" Paul asked, unsure of how to help since he didn't know what he was looking for.

"Possibly. It can't be a coincidence that this message seems vaguely familiar, and then suddenly I remember some old book about the ancient world from years ago. Ah-ha! Here it is!"

Jarod pulled out what appeared to be an old children's picture book. The cover had seen better days, battered and rumpled, covered in decades of dust. He cleared most of it to reveal it's title: 'A Children's Guide to Ancient Lands' and brought it over to the dining table to examine.

"I had this book when I was in primary school. My parents gave it to me when I expressed interest in Ancient Egypt and Hieroglyphics. I have a theory about the message, and if I'm right, this book will be the key to proving it."

"What do you want me to do with the rest of these books and boxes, boss?" Troy asked, looking around at the cluttered mess on the floor.

"If there's any free space in the library room, transfer the books in there. Anything that won't fit can be boxed up and put back under the bed."

"Alright. Are you going to be working today, or are you off to the police station again?" Troy asked, eyeing Paul and sounding vaguely amused.

Had Jarod told Troy about what happened last night?

"I'm taking a few days off. Just while I'm working with the detectives on this translation. In the meantime, you can take a few days off too, if you like. Call it paid leave."

Troy looked like he was about to jump for joy. "Seriously? Paid time off? Say no more, boss! You take as much time off as you need. I'm always happy to support your endeavours to pay me for sitting on my pert little bum," he said with a cheeky grin.

"Don't you or your pert little bum get too excited. I'll still need you to keep on top of the email account. Let any clients that get in contact know that we are closed for a few days. You know the routine."

"No worries. I can do that from my phone while I'm soaking up the sun on the beach at St Kilda. Thanks, boss!" Troy suddenly grabbed Jarod in an unexpected embrace, kissing him on the cheek.

"You're not on holiday yet, Troy! Get the books sorted out first. Then you can sun yourself." Jarod placed the children's book in his messenger bag, grabbed his keys, phone and wallet, then headed for the door.

"I'm ready to go when you are," Jarod announced to Paul. Paul opened the door and allowed Jarod to walk ahead of him. He gave Troy a curt nod goodbye, then closed the door behind them.

~

On the way to the station, Paul is acutely aware of Jarod's proximity. Every time they are in the car together, a kind of sensory overload hits him without warning. Jarod's mild aftershave fills the air, and it's all Paul can do not to pull over on the side of the road and bury his nose in Jarod's neck. But he pulls himself together. Paul didn't know what it was about Jarod that made him lose control, but he wasn't going to let it happen again. Especially when they have to work together.

Besides which, he was a little shocked at just how forceful he had been when he had kissed Jarod. The cockiness and bravado that had him swaggering out of Jarod's apartment last night had evaporated, leaving Paul feeling like a brute. He hadn't been gentle. He hadn't even asked Jarod if it was okay to kiss him. What if Jarod was upset about it? He'd be quite within his rights to make a formal complaint about Paul's actions last night. He needed to address this immediately.

"I wanted to apologise about last night," Paul eventually said, breaking the awkward silence, "I should have..."

"No need to apologise. I completely understand."

"You do?" Paul was puzzled.

"Your work is important. I wasn't offended that you needed to cancel our dinner plans." Jarod said calmly.

"Um, thanks. I'm glad you understand how important my work is. But that wasn't what I was talking about. I shouldn't have kissed you like that. Not without asking first. Plus, in the middle of this case. I was out of line."

"I'll admit, I wasn't expecting you to kiss me, but I didn't object. It made me... I'm not sure how to describe it. I... felt something."

Paul's chest puffed up with pride. Somehow, his kiss had created a crack in the ice shield that surrounded Jarod's heart. Paul knew it was a neanderthal response, but he just couldn't help but take pride in knowing he had somehow effected Jarod.

"Did it feel good?" Paul asked hesitantly, hoping the answer was yes.

"I... enjoyed the sensation. I don't know how or why I felt what I felt, but it wasn't unpleasant. It's the first time I've experienced a major emotional reaction since the accident. I wonder what it means?"

Paul desperately tried not to smirk. Jarod's rather cold description of how their kiss had touched him was far from high praise, but considering his circumstances, perhaps it was.

"Maybe it means you like me?" Paul offered gently.

"Perhaps..." Jarod said absently. He seemed distracted suddenly.

Paul pulled into the underground carpark at the police station and escorted Jarod upstairs to the Homicide department. Jarod headed straight to the conference room while Paul went to his desk to check in with Bryce and go over any paperwork that had come in overnight.

After he left Jarod's apartment the previous evening, Paul had made some discreet inquiries into Justin Porter's whereabouts for the night of Clarissa's murder. His employer confirmed that Justin was in his office at Crayborn Financial Services where he works as a financial trader. Witnesses and CCTV footage confirmed his alibi.

Even still, Paul still found Justin's sudden appearance at Jarod's apartment after so many years, and his subsequent outbursts and accusations, highly suspicious. He couldn't shake the feeling that something about Justin's behaviour seemed 'off' somehow. But with a solid alibi, he was clearly not the killer.

Paul was jostled from his thoughts when Jarod appeared by his side. He was holding the children's book.

"Guys, I've translated the symbols."

"Really? What do they say?" Bryce stood up excitedly.

"You should come and see for yourselves. I'm not sure what to make of it."

With that, Jarod turned away and headed back to the conference room. Bryce following close behind, with Paul bringing up the rear. As he entered the glass room, he looked over at the large whiteboard onto which Jarod had transcribed the symbols. Underneath in large, red letters was the English translation:

'HAVE I GOT YOUR ATTENTION YET'

Chapter 9

AS SOON AS Jarod had laid eyes on the dusty old children's book in his apartment, he had instinctively known it was the key to decoding the symbols. But it wasn't until he turned to the back of the book, he found his instincts to be dead on.

"How did a children's book help you decode the symbols when all your other notebooks didn't?" Paul asked, his eyes never moving from the whiteboard.

"Because the notebooks only cover languages. This..." Jarod held up the children's book, "...has a section on puzzles."

"Puzzles?" Bryce looked confused.

"In the back of the book, there is an activity section. Crosswords, find-a-words, that sort of thing. All based on the information in the book. Amongst all these activities, there is also a coded message puzzle using Cuneiform characters."

Jarod flipped through the pages and opened the book to the section featuring a grid of symbols similar to the ones drawn on Clarissa's wall.

"Each symbol represents a letter of the alphabet. It's only a simple substitution code, but this book was written for children. There's even a code key at the bottom of the page, so the reader can come up with there own coded messages."

"And this code matches the message from Clarissa's?" Paul asked.

"To the letter. I haven't seen this book since I was a child. I'd completely forgotten about it. It wasn't until I started trying to translate the symbols, that my long term memory started churning. Now I remember reading this book as a kid, doing the puzzles and even making up my own coded messages. I knew there was something familiar about the symbols. Now I know why."

Paul and Bryce looked at each other as if silently communicating with one another. Jarod wasn't sure what to make of that.

"Well done, Jarod. I was beginning to wonder if we would ever get a break in this case. Now we have it." Bryce said, giving Jarod a sharp slap on the shoulder.

"I'm not sure how much of a break it is. The message doesn't really reveal anything." Jarod was hoping the translation would yield something more helpful.

"It gives us a lot to go on," Paul countered, "Now that we know what kind of code it is, that could help tell us something about the killer. We can try and trace the book. See if anyone has bought a copy recently or checked it out of a library. The message itself may have some meaning to Clarissa's family or one of the other people in her life that we've spoken to already. You've been a tremendous help. This might be just what we need to catch this guy."

Jarod was glad he had been helpful, but despite Paul's gushing praise, he questioned how much use the book or the decoded message would be in catching a killer. But then again, he wasn't a police detective. Chances were, Paul and Bryce knew better than anyone what was a hot lead and what was a dead end.

"Who do you think this message was for? The victim?" Bryce asked no one in particular.

"That's hardly likely. Clarissa would have been dead or dying when the killer was writing it. If the killer had something to say to her, painting it on the wall in her blood wasn't the most straight forward way of doing it." Jarod blurted out.

Paul's facial expression became tense. Perhaps he was frowning. Either way, he was directing it at Jarod.

I did it again. I blurted out something inappropriate.

"I apologise, Bryce. I can't censor myself much these days. I meant no disrespect."

Bryce nodded sharply.

"It's possibly a message to the police," Paul suggested, "A taunt of some kind. It could also be a message to Clarissa's family."

"That doesn't make much sense either," Jarod said.

"Why's that?"

"Well, in both cases, neither the police nor Clarissa's family could read the message without me decoding it, and the killer couldn't have known I would be able to decode it. I didn't even know I could decode it."

Once again, the two detectives looked at each other and did that silent communication thing. Jarod was beginning to dislike that but continued with his thoughts.

"If the killer was directing the message at a specific person or persons, wouldn't they write it in a way the intended recipient could actually read? Unless of course, the coded message was for me?"

"That's unlikely," Paul said dismissively, "As you said, how would the killer know you could actually translate it? How would they even know you had the book?"

Jarod had to agree with Paul on that. The children's book had been boxed up with a bunch of other childhood books and knick-knacks, under his bed, for several years now. Before that, it had been in storage at his parent's house prior to them selling up and moving to Canada.

"I'm going to look into the book angle. See if I can find us a lead that way. Find out how many copies are out there. If it's widely available. Recent sales or library borrows. This could take a while." Bryce sighed and took the book from Jarod. He placed it in a transparent evidence bag, then left the conference room and headed back to his desk.

Jarod began packing up his notebooks and materials. With the translation complete, there was no further reason for him to remain at the police station. He should really get back home and focus on work. Troy, despite his excitement at some paid time off, seemed a little off-put at suspending operations. Jarod had to remember that his assistant had a schedule too, and despite his lighthearted attitude, Troy was as much a stickler for routine as he was.

"Before you go," Paul said, "I need you to write up a statement covering everything you know about the book, the symbols and how you decoded the message. It's just routine. I'd like to have everything on file so we have all our bases covered when we catch this guy and go to trial."

"Certainly. I'll start right now." Jarod said as he finished packing his things into a large cardboard box on the conference table. He accepted a pad and pen from Paul, sat down on one of the chairs and began writing out everything he knew.

Jarod went into excruciating detail, not wanting to leave out a single detail. He knew the importance of comprehensive notes and wanted to make sure Paul had everything he needed. After almost two hours, Jarod's statement totalled over thirty pages. He signed and initialled each page and bound them together with a sturdy paperclip he found in amongst the office supplies in the conference room. With nothing left to do, Jarod picked up the heavy box of notebooks and walked out to Paul's desk to deliver his statement.

Paul appeared to be compiling a list of people to reinterview, while Bryce was on the phone, his expression was unreadable.

"Here you go. I tried to be as detailed as possible, but if you need more, just let me know and I can rewrite it."

Paul's eyes bulged when Jarod handed him the thick wad of papers.

"No, I think this will be fine," he said with a chuckle, "But I'll let you know if I need anything more. You look like you're ready to go?"

"I think I have everything."

"Well, how about I take you to lunch, then I'll drop you off home?"

"I am feeling a little peckish. After you, detective."

The two men grabbed their things and headed across the office, but just as they reached the lifts, a loud whistle caught their attention. Jarod turned to see Bryce calling them back.

"Sorry mate, lunch is cancelled," Bryce said, "There's been another murder. First responders describe the scene as being similar to the Wainwright murder."

"Damn it," Paul said under his breath, "Where?"

Bryce was silent for a moment. He looked at Jarod, then directed his gaze at Paul. Jarod wasn't sure what that expression was meant to convey, but Jarod felt the hairs on the back of his neck stand up.

"I'm sorry, Paul. It's at Justin Porter's apartment."

Chapter 10

PAUL ARRANGED FOR one of the uniformed officers to drive Jarod home. Upon hearing the news of Justin's murder, Paul could have sworn Jarod, despite his ever-present cool and stoic exterior, lost a little of the light in his eyes. Perhaps he wasn't so unaffected by his emotions as he thought. Paul resolved himself to stop by Jarod's place on his way home from work to check in on him, presuming he finished at a reasonable hour.

Paul wasn't sure how to react to the news of Justin Porter's death. Despite having dated briefly a few months earlier, the two men were never really that close. As a homicide detective, Paul had learned to detach himself emotionally from the cases he worked on. It was an essential skill in his line of work. He couldn't afford to be guided by any feelings of grief or loss. Any such emotional indulgences could compromise his objectivity. Being able to set aside his own feelings was also the only way of maintaining his sanity when working day after day in a world filled with so much viciousness and cruelty. But he couldn't ignore that, as a regular human being, he was finding it difficult to suppress how awful he felt about finding out someone he knew had been brutally killed.

For the briefest of moments, Paul almost envied Jarod and his emotional detachment. He sort of understood what Jarod had said about being able to better focus on his work without the impediment or distraction of feelings.

Let it go for now. I need to concentrate on the case.

Upon discovering his personal connection to Justin Porter, Paul's superiors attempted to remove him from the case. They felt that his presence during the investigation could be seen as a serious conflict of interest. However, since he had a solid alibi for the time of the murder, there was no conceivable legal conflict. He was also able to successfully argue that his connection to Justin was at best minimal since their relationship had been so short-lived and that he wouldn't have a problem working objectively with Bryce to solve the case. Reluctantly, they had agreed, but Paul knew he was standing on very shaky ground with his bosses, and that he couldn't afford to screw up this case.

Justin lived in the Esplanade building, a recently constructed luxury tower in the heart of the newly redeveloped Docklands district. With its harbour views and multi-million dollar price tags, this was the home of Melbourne's young urban professional elites. His apartment was on the twenty-fourth floor, and Paul didn't want to ask how much it had set the successful financial trader back. Sufficed to say, it was well outside of Paul's price range.

When Paul and Bryce arrived at Justin's apartment, they were confronted by a similar scene to what they had encountered at the Wainwright scene. Paul had visited Justin's place only once previously. The apartment was large, modern and fastidiously neat. It was almost like nothing had changed during the ensuing months. Everything was exactly as he remembered. Except for the kitchen.

Justin's body, which lay bloody and brutalised on the kitchen floor, had been discovered by his workmate, Mike Bradshaw, who was waiting outside to be interviewed. He had only met Mikey, as he preferred to be addressed, once briefly when Paul and Justin had met up for drinks at some nightclub. Paul wasn't much for clubbing but had pretended to enjoy himself at the time. Mikey had seemed like a nice enough guy.

According to the medical examiner on the scene, his initial examination of the victim's body suggested he had been struck in the back of the head with a blunt, heavy object, then stabbed at least twelve times with a kitchen knife. The knife was found next to the body and had been taken from the kitchen by the killer. Time of death was estimated to be approximately seven pm the previous evening.

Interesting. Justin wasn't stabbed as much as Clarissa. Is that significant?

There was no doubt in Paul's mind that this was the work of the same killer. The two crime scenes were virtually identical. Once again, the victim's blood had been used to paint crude symbols on the wall. Similar in style to the first crime scene, but clearly a different message. Paul pulled out his phone and took a quick photo of the symbols. Hopefully, now that Jarod had successfully translated the symbol code, this new message from the killer would present them with a valuable clue. He would show the new symbols to Jarod as soon as he could.

With nothing more they could do until the M.E. and forensics team got their final reports in, Bryce and Paul left the crime scene techs to their work, stepped outside of the apartment and began their preliminary interview with Mikey Bradshaw. The young man was sitting on the floor in the corridor, his face a study in grief and shock. His face was blotchy and tear-streaked, and his eyes were bloodshot from weeping.

"Mr Bradshaw," Bryce began gently, "I'm Detective Bryce Gordon. This is my partner Detective Paul Kincaid. Melbourne City Homicide. We'd like to ask you a few questions if you're feeling up to it."

Mikey nodded ever so slightly and quickly wiped his face on his sleeve. He stood up and faced the two detectives.

"Paul? Oh my god, I thought it was you. I can't believe this is happening."

"Mr Bradshaw, can you tell us what happened?" Bryce's tone was a little firmer than before. Mikey directed his attention to the other detective.

"Of course. I'm sorry. Justin didn't show up for work this morning. We work together at Crayborn Financial Services. I thought maybe he was sick or something, but he didn't respond to any of my texts or calls. It seemed a little unusual, so I thought I'd drop in during my lunch break to make sure he was okay."

"What happened then?" Paul asked, furiously scribbling notes on his notepad.

"When I knocked, there was no answer. So I used his spare key. Justin gave it to me in case of emergencies. I looked around the apartment and it seemed like he wasn't home. But then I walked into the kitchen and..." Bradshaw stopped, unable to stop the well of tears that burst forth.

"Take your time. There's no rush." Paul said soothingly.

"There was just blood everywhere. And his face. His eyes just staring at me. It was horrible. I'll never forget it as long as I live."

"Did you notice anything unusual in the apartment. Anything out of place or missing?" Bryce asked.

Mikey considered this for a moment, "I don't think so. Everything seemed to be as it always is. Justin is... was... a bit of a neat freak. He didn't like things being moved or put out of place."

"Had Justin recently mentioned anything about being threatened? Did he seem unusually nervous or scared?" Paul asked, wondering if their killer had been stalking his victims.

"No. Justin seemed fine. He never mentioned any threats to me. In fact, he'd been really happy recently. He was up for a big promotion at work. Justin was certain he was going to get it." Mikey pulled a handkerchief out of this pocket and blew his nose.

"Do you know if anyone at work held a grudge against him? Perhaps someone who would want Justin out of the way so they could get that promotion?" Bryce asked a little bluntly. Paul frowned at him.

"Well, we're financial traders. We're all a little ruthless, but not like that. I can't imagine anyone going so far as to kill Justin just to snag a promotion. Although, you never know. It's a cutthroat business, and it's amazing how nasty our petty little rivalries can get."

"Perhaps you could put together a list of your colleagues at work? People who might be up for the same promotion as Justin. People who were his work rivals. It might help lead us to Justin's killer." Bryce said, handing over his notepad and pen. Mikey took them and began slowly writing down a series of names.

"I'm going to start interviewing the neighbours. Maybe someone heard or saw something." Paul said to Bryce, who nodded his agreement.

"Paul, wait!" Mikey said, and Paul turned back to face him.

"You're going to catch this bastard, aren't you? You're gonna get the sick fuck that did this to Justin?"

"We'll do our best," Paul said solemnly. What else could he say? He couldn't make any lofty promises at this point. With a sharp nod, he turned around and Paul left Mikey with Bryce.

~

None of the neighbours saw or heard anything unusual. No strangers hanging around. No loud noises or screams. Nothing. Worse still, despite being a luxury building, security was ludicrously inadequate. There were no interior CCTV, and the external security cameras were of low quality and poorly placed. Even if the killer hadn't known the layout of the building, they could have easily eluded the cameras without even trying.

Paul was frustrated. With little to go on, for now, Bryce decided to return to the station, while Paul would head over to Jarod's place and hopefully get a translation on the new symbol message. Bryce dropped him off at the Paradiso on his way through.

"Do you want me to swing back and pick you up later?" Bryce asked.

"Nah, mate. I'll get a cab from here. It's getting late in the day anyway. You should head on home. We'll pick it up fresh in the morning."

"Agreed. See you in the morning." Bryce gave him a weary nod, then drove away.

Paul climbed the stairs to Jarod's apartment and knocked on his door. Moments later, the door opened. Jarod had changed his clothes into something more casual: a worn pair of jeans and an old t-shirt that looked soft and comfortable.

"I wasn't expecting to see you again tonight. Is everything okay?"

"May I come in?"

"Certainly." Jarod stepped aside and allowed Paul entry.

The living room was softly lit with warm lamplight. A cup of tea was sitting on the coffee table next to a hefty book that Jarod was apparently in the middle of reading.

"Would you like something to drink?" Jarod offered, but Paul declined.

"I've just been at Justin's apartment. So far, it looks like he was murdered by the same person as your neighbour."

Jarod appeared to subtly shake at this revelation. It was subtle, almost imperceptible, but Paul saw it.

"Are you okay?"

"I have to admit, finding out two people I know have been brutally killed in a matter of days is... uncomfortable. But otherwise, I'm fine. I spent most of the afternoon working on a new translation for a client, so I haven't really had much time to think about it."

"There was another coded message left at Justin's apartment. Written in blood. Would you be willing to take a look at the symbols?"

"If it's written in the same code, I should be able to translate it immediately. I have the substitution code committed to memory now."

Paul pulled out his phone and opened up the photos app. He found the appropriate image and handed the device over to Jarod. He examined the photo carefully, zooming in and out to get a better view of the symbols.

"Is it the same code?" Paul asked.

"Yes. It appears to be the same."

"What does it day?"

Jarod was silent for a moment, his brows knitting together in concentration.

"It says... 'You forced me to do this.' "

Chapter 11

JAROD WAS VAGUELY aware of Paul's voice in the background, the detective calling his partner to relay the news of the latest symbol translation. Beyond that, Jarod wasn't really aware of anything else. He was too busy trying to process everything.

Two people he knew had been senselessly murdered in a matter of days. Their killer was a madman leaving macabre and cryptic messages written in blood. In that moment, Jarod simply couldn't make sense of it all. So many questions swirled through his head.

What did the messages mean? Did they actually have a meaning? Who are the messages intended for? Are the victims random or were they selected for a reason?

Jarod had a hard time believing that two people from his life would be savagely killed only days apart purely by coincidence. But how were they connected? He found it even harder to believe that a financial trader and old age pensioner would have many common links or be part of the same social groups. Clarissa wasn't exactly a high flying, wealthy professional, and Jarod found it unlikely that Justin spent much of his free time down at the senior citizen's centre playing cards or participating in the senior's choir.

Beyond himself, Jarod couldn't think of a single thing that connected the two of them.

Beyond himself.

Paul had just finished his call to Bryce and noticed Jarod frozen to the spot, deep in thought.

"Are you okay?" Paul asked gently.

"It's me."

"What are you talking about?"

"It's me. I'm the connection. It's the only thing that fits."

Paul's eyebrows scrunched together. Jarod figured he was confused, or possibly angry. He couldn't be sure.

"Clarissa and Justin. They weren't killed at random. So there has to be a connection. So what do they have in common? Me. I'm the common denominator. I knew them both. Beyond that, they have no connection whatsoever."

"Hold your horses, sweetheart," Paul said, placing his hands on Jarod's shoulders and squeezing gently, "I think you're jumping the gun a little. It's way too early in the investigation to be drawing any conclusions about the killer's motivations."

"But it makes sense!" Jarod said, his voice rising ever so slightly.

"Not really. We don't know enough about this killer to be able to draw any conclusions on his motivation. For all we know, he did pick them at random. It could just be a coincidence that they have you in common. The first rule of murder investigations is 'Don't jump to conclusions.' Until we gather more conclusive evidence, we can't be certain of anything."

Jarod had a hard time believing that, but he deferred to the detective's judgement. Clearly, he had more experience with these matters. Deciding he wanted a break from all this murder and mayhem, Jarod returned to his cup of tea but found it had gone cold.

"I'm making some more tea. Are you sure I can't interest you in a cup of coffee?" Jarod enquired as he picked up his cup and saucer and headed toward the kitchen.

"Okay, a coffee would be nice. Thanks." Paul said with a broad smile, which was reminiscent of the smile he had been sporting just after he had kissed Jarod.

Is he going to kiss me again?

Jarod considered Paul's kiss from the other night while he made the tea and coffee. His reaction to it had been unexpected. On reflection, he tried to put a name to the feeling he had experienced, and the only one that seemed to fit was 'excitement' - a kind of mild, but not unsubstantial thrill. His heart rate had increased and his breathing had accelerated.

Jarod didn't have a lot of experience with kissing, sex or romance in general. The rare, fumbling encounters he had experienced before the accident had been few and far between, and he had difficulty remembering what they had felt like. The fact that Paul's kiss had provoked any kind of emotional reaction at all had been genuinely surprising. Perhaps his doctors had been correct, about his brain eventually rewiring itself, after all?

But Jarod knew better than anyone about leaping to conclusions when it came to neurological episodes. It didn't mean he was going to suddenly be returned to full cognitive function. The occasional random emotional outburst may be all he is ever capable of experiencing. Pinning his hopes on some miracle recovery would be foolhardy.

He had gotten used to his condition. He wasn't even sure he would want to 'recover' after all this time. His condition might have some drawbacks, but it also had a lot of positive benefits. It had taken years for Jarod to adapt and get used to his new circumstances. It would be... inconvenient to have to go through all that again.

But that kiss was exciting.

The experience of Paul thrusting him up against that door. Paul's lips pressed to his own. That unexpected rush of sensation as that spike of electricity sparked between them.

"What's got you blushing?" Paul asked smoothly, interrupting Jarod's wool-gathering.

"I was just thinking about you kissing me, and how it made me feel excited when you did it." Jarod blurted out without a moment's thought.

Paul chuckled and slowly approached him, stalking into his space.

"Would you like me to kiss you again?"

Jarod turned to Paul, looked up into his eyes and quietly nodded his agreement. He was curious to see if another kiss would have the same effect on him, or if the first time was just a random synaptic misfire or fluke. Paul wrapped his thick, muscular arms around him and drew him close so they were chest to chest.

"I haven't finished making your coffee yet," Jarod said.

"Forget about the coffee."

And with that, Paul pressed their lips together. Gently at first, teasing, exploring. His tongue carefully sliding along Jarod's upper lip, requesting admittance. Jarod opened for him and Paul deepened the kiss. Jarod felt tingly all over as Paul gently probed his mouth, allowing their tongues to slide together slowly and languidly.

Jarod used his hands to explore Paul's broad shoulders and back. Just touching his hard, defined muscles seemed to increase the all over sensations he was experiencing, making him feel giddy. This was better than the last kiss. It was more intense. Paul emitted a low, rumbling growl as he gently used his teeth to tug at Jarod's lower lip. Jarod whimpered unexpectedly, and he could feel Paul's hardness pressing insistently against him. Jarod broke the kiss and sucked in a deep breath.

"Are you okay?"

"That was... intense. I wasn't expecting that." Jarod said as he gulped in precious air.

"Perhaps you should make an appointment with your doctor if you're feeling out of sorts."

"I'm not sick. I'm just not used to this. You make me feel things. Things I've never felt before. Things I didn't know I could feel."

A medical opinion might be needed in the future. The fact that he was starting to feel any kind of emotional reactions was clearly something that needed to be investigated. But it was hardly an emergency. At least, not quite yet.

"It feels different for me too. I've never felt like this with anyone else, Jarod. You're very special to me."

"You're special to me too. I've never met anyone like you. You make me... I don't have the words. Will you stay with me tonight, Paul?"

"I'd love to, sweetheart. And, maybe you and I don't need words..." Paul said as he held Jarod's head with both hands and brought their lips together again.

Chapter 12

EVENTUALLY, PAUL BROKE off the kiss, allowing both men to breathe again, and Jarod resumed making their drinks in the kitchen. Paul headed back to the softly lit living room and sat down on the sofa. He couldn't have wiped the smug smile off his face if he tried.

Considering Jarod's neurological condition, and his general emotional neutrality, it was hard for Paul not to feel a little cocky and self-satisfied knowing that just a simple kiss from him was enough to melt through Jarod's cool exterior.

Yeah, I'm an arrogant neanderthal. But damn, that was a hot kiss!

When he had deepened the kiss and held Jarod in his arms, Paul could almost envision the chips of ice falling away from the smaller man's thawing heart. Paul briefly wondered if a few had fallen away from his own heart, too.

He'd never felt such an instant physical connection to someone before. Being attracted to someone is one thing, as is being turned on by them. But when their lips touched for the first time, Paul felt something more; something deeper. It was like he had found the other half of himself. A half he hadn't known was missing until that very moment. It was exhilarating, but also a little scary.

Jarod was special. Paul didn't want to lose him, just as he had every other man he'd tried to form a relationship with. But despite his fears and insecurities, he also felt hope. Hope that this time, things would be different.

Jarod returned to the living room baring two mugs. He handed one to Paul, a steaming milky coffee, then sat in his usual chair with his tea.

"Why don't you come sit over here with me?" Paul patted the sofa cushion next to him.

Jarod looked momentarily confused. Paul had deduced that he was a creature of habit. Jarod liked routines and schedules and order. It probably never occurred to him to sit next to the man he had just been passionately kissing. Eventually, Jarod stood up, placed his tea on the coffee table, and tentatively sat down next to Paul. He placed his hand on Jarod's shoulder and gave it a gentle, reassuring squeeze.

"There, that's better, isn't it?"

"I don't usually sit here, but it's pleasant enough."

"It certainly is..." Paul said gently as he leaned in and planted soft, featherlight kisses behind Jarod's ear and down his neck. Jarod instinctively inclined his head, granting more access, and Paul found that sweet spot on Jarod's throat. He began sucking on it, grazing his teeth along the tender skin. Jarod gasped quietly, betraying his cool exterior once again.

"That feels... I don't know how to describe that. It's fascinating."

Paul smirked. Jarod appeared to be enjoying his attentions, and Paul really enjoyed the fact it was kind of scattering Jarod's usually cool persona.

"So tell me, sweetheart. Why did you ask me to stay with you tonight?"

Jarod turned slightly to face him. He looked deep into Paul's eyes with laser focus.

"I was wondering if you would be interested in having some sort of sex with me?"

'Some sort of sex with me'

Jarod's flirtation skills were rusty, or possibly damaged in transit. But Paul found his rather abrupt bluntness rather endearing.

"I'd..." Paul tried to find the words, "I'd love that."

"I just want to be clear. I'm not making any promises. I'm not even sure how this would work. Or even if it could work. I don't know how functional I am in that department. I didn't have much experience before the accident, and I never really considered the idea of sexual activity since. But then I met you, and things... feel... different. And..."

Paul cut him off with another searing kiss. Deep and possessive, he pulled Jarod into his lap and held him closely.

"Relax, sweetheart. We don't have to rush into anything. We can take things one step at a time. Let's focus on what feels good, and go from there. Okay?"

Jarod nodded. With their crotches lined up, Paul could feel Jarod's hardness against his. Jarod was at least partially 'functional' as he had so eloquently put it. Paul once again began kissing and nibbling on Jarod's delicate neck. Jarod's hips suddenly began to move, grinding and rubbing, creating the most delicious friction. Paul's breath became ragged as the two men moved together.

Jarod grabbed Paul's head with both hands and took control of a warm, powerful kiss that had Paul's toes curling. Usually, Paul was the more dominant partner when it came down to things. But the way Jarod was grinding against him and kissing the life out of him, he just went with it and let the smaller man explore.

Before long, they were each approaching the edge, their breathing synchronised and hearts beating hard enough to burst through their ribcages. Paul grabbed hold of Jarod's hips, guiding their movements as they reached their climax. Jarod let out a moan that was soft yet ever so primal as every muscle in Paul's body went rigid, his release overpowering him. Jarod stiffened at the same moment and collapsed onto his chest, heaving in deep breaths and kissing his neck.

"Are you okay, sweetheart?" Paul asked tentatively once his heartbeat levelled out.

"Yes."

"How was that for you?"

"It was... good."

"Seemed like it was more than good." Paul chuckled.

"It was...very good." Jarod clarified.

"Well, I thought it was very good too."

Paul stood up, carrying Jarod in his arms and took them both into the bathroom to clean up.

"We made a bit of a mess," Jarod said mildly.

"Yeah, but it was worth it."

"It was."

The two men stripped, showered and changed. Paul borrowed a large pair of Jarod's workout shorts. They were a little snug but would do for sleeping in. He quickly washed up his clothes and hung them up to dry on the shower rail. They would be fine by morning.

"Let's get into bed and get some sleep. I have a feeling tomorrow is going to be a busy day." Paul said as he guided Jarod to the bedroom.

They quickly got under the covers, Paul snuggling up behind Jarod, and they quickly drifted into a calm, sated sleep.

Chapter 13

THE NEXT MORNING, Jarod awoke just before the alarm feeling rested and refreshed. He switched off the alarm so as not to disturb Paul, who was still sleeping soundly next to him in bed. Jarod carefully untangled himself from the bed covers and Paul's arms, got out of bed and quietly stepped into the bathroom.

After freshening up, Jarod headed to the kitchen to make himself some tea. As the kettle started to boil, Paul emerged from the bedroom looking like a rumpled zombie. Jarod immediately grabbed a second mug and began preparing a strong cup of coffee, for which Paul spoons him from behind and gently kisses his neck in gratitude.

"Morning, sweetheart," Paul said with a rough, sleepy voice.

"Morning. Sorry if I woke you. I tried not to disturb you."

"You could never disturb me. Besides, I needed to get up soon. I have to head home, get changed and head into the station."

Jarod finished up their drinks and handed the coffee over to Paul, who held the mug with both hands like it were a precious object that needed to be cradled and kept safe at all costs.

Jarod was still trying to sort out how he felt about the events of last night, specifically the feelings part. Paul seemed to be able to inspire emotions in him that had been absent since the accident. He was out of practice when it came to emotional reactions, so he was having a lot of difficulties identifying them with any degree of accuracy.

Last night had been his first sexual experience since the accident, with the exception of masturbation. And frankly, the two events did not compare. Ever since he had sustained his brain injury, masturbation had been a bland, mechanical experience. It was purely a physical act, specifically for the purpose of 'clearing the pipes' so to speak. There had been no emotions or pleasurable sensations; merely a relief of pressure. For Jarod, touching himself intimately had been no more an erotic experience than blowing his nose.

Last night had been different. It had felt... good. Kissing Paul had felt exciting, but the feeling of rubbing their bodies together had felt so much more powerful. His breathing and heartbeat had gone haywire, and his body had tingled like he had touched a live wire.

Overall, the experience had been positive. But it had also left Jarod concerned. He was preoccupied, not by the happening itself, but the feelings he had experienced as a result. He was preoccupied that he was preoccupied.

What does this mean? Is my brain regenerating? Will I change again? How will I cope?

Jarod had fully accepted a life without feeling things, and in many ways, his lack of emotions had been a blessing. He didn't get depressed. He didn't get lonely. He didn't get jealous or angry or scared. He had excellent focus and wasn't easily distracted. In many respects, he was better and more productive than he had ever been before. But a simple hug from Paul was all it took to shake something loose deep inside of him. Jarod wasn't so sure that was a good thing.

"Hey," Paul said, snapping Jarod out of his thoughts, "It's too early in the morning to be thinking so hard."

"Can't help it. My brain starts and there's no stopping it."

"Well, we'll see about that." Paul stepped into his personal space and laid another deep, powerful kiss on him. Jarod's mind went blank as he melted into Paul's arms and surrendered to the moment.

As they sat and sipped their drinks, Paul asked what Jarod's plans for the day were.

"I'm going to visit Clarissa's daughter to offer my condolences. I also want to ensure her son gets the book about Ancient Egypt. Hopefully, it's not too late for his project."

"I don't like the idea of you going anywhere on your own at the moment. Not while this maniac is on the loose."

Jarod scoffed. "There's no conceivable danger. The killer attacks people in their own home. If anything, going out would probably be safer than staying here."

Paul's expression was tight. He was probably frustrated that he couldn't argue with Jarod's logic.

"Well, be careful. Call me immediately if you notice anything unusual, or if for any reason you don't feel safe. I mean it. I don't want anything to happen to you."

Paul's tone was hard and serious. Jarod felt a slight flutter in his stomach. Like the butterflies from the other day.

I should probably have something to eat.

"Shall I make some toast? Do you have time for breakfast?"

"I better go get changed and head off, but some toast would be nice. I'll eat it in the car. Thanks, sweetheart." Paul kissed him on his forehead and headed into the bathroom to get dressed.

Jarod made some cinnamon toast for them both, placing some on a plate for himself and a few slices in a paper bag for Paul. By the time Paul emerged from the bathroom, the apartment was filled with the aroma of non-dairy spread and cinnamon sugar.

"Here's you go. Have a nice day at work." Jarod said, offering the paper bag to Paul, who accepted it with a wide smile and kissed him deeply in gratitude.

"Stay safe. I'll talk to you later."

"Yes, detective."

~

When the tram arrived around the corner from Elizabeth's house, it was just after ten am. The mid-morning sun was warm but gentle, and a light breeze carried the scent of wildflowers from the nearby public park. Jarod got off the tram and walked the short distance to the small Federation style home that Elizabeth Wainwright shared with her son.

The house, which according to Clarissa, had been acquired as part of Elizabeth's divorce settlement some years ago. The front yard was small but neat, with garden beds filled with blooming lilacs on either side of the concrete path leading up to the front door. Jarod rang the doorbell and waited patiently for a response. The door opened after a short delay, revealing a statuesque woman in her early forties. Her long, blonde hair was arranged in a hurried ponytail, and her outfit suggested she had been in the backyard gardening.

"May I help you?"

"Good morning. I'm Jarod Cruickshank."

"Jarod? Oh, Mum's friend? I was hoping to speak to you. Please, do come in." Elizabeth stepped aside and allowed Jarod entry.

"You're too kind."

Jarod stepped into a long hallway lit by a single, large skylight. The walls were decorated with framed photographs, presumably of family or friends. Elizabeth ushered him into a spacious living room to the left. They sat down on a large, overstuffed sofa with fluffy grey cushions.

"Can I offer you something to drink?"

"I'm fine, thank you. I wanted to offer my condolences. Your mother and I knew each other for a long time, and I'm so sorry for your loss."

"Thank you, Jarod. Mum spoke of you often. She was always telling me about the kind young man across the hall who would look out for her. Thank you so much for doing that."

"To be honest, I think it was more of your mother looking out for me, whether I wanted her to or not. I suspect when she found out about my brain injury, her mothering instinct kicked in and she felt the need to keep a watchful eye on me."

"Yeah, that sounds like Mum." Elizabeth forced a brittle smile. She had clearly been devastated by recent events. Jarod, not for the first time, was grateful he was unable to feel the grief Clarissa's daughter was experiencing.

"I… understand you were the one to find her…" Elizabeth said hesitantly.

"Yes. I was concerned because she hadn't come over to my apartment as expected."

She nodded absently.

"That's part of the reason I'm here," Jarod opened his messenger bag and pulled out the book on Ancient Egypt, "I understand your son wanted to borrow this for his school assignment."

Jarod handed the heavy tome over, and Elizabeth accepted it with wide eyes. She began to tear up and she dabbed her eyes with a scrunched up tissue from her pocket.

"I'm sorry. Did I do something wrong? I'm not good at judging emotions. Did I offend you?"

"No! No, you didn't. This is just so kind of you. Thank you so much for going to all this trouble. I haven't told Riley the full details of his grandmother's death. I don't think he's old enough to handle it. But this will be perfect for his assignment. Just the distraction he needs at the moment. Thank you so much."

"You're very welcome. It was the least I could do."

"I don't understand why anyone would do this. Why would someone want to hurt Mum? She was harmless." Elizabeth said through tears.

"I have no idea. Did your mother ever express concerns about anyone? Maybe, somebody she argued with or didn't get along with?"

"No. Not really. The only person she ever had harsh words for was my ex-husband. He was a fly-in-fly-out worker in a mine in Western Australia. Towards the end of our marriage, we only saw him for a couple of days a month. Mum hated it, and would constantly complain about my 'absentee husband' and how it wasn't good for Riley."

"Do you think your ex-husband harboured any resentment towards your mother?"

"Bill? Nah! He was the most easy-going man I ever met. Besides, he lives in the United Arab Emirates now. Working for some big oil company. No chance he was involved."

Jarod thought it was worth getting Paul to look into her ex-husband's whereabouts nonetheless, and filed that away for later.

"Did your mother ever mention any strangers coming into her home? Maybe door-to-door salesmen or tradies?"

"I don't think so. But then again, most of the time Mum was too busy telling me about all the latest gossip from the senior's centre."

Yeah, I can relate to that. Clarissa was infamous for her gossip updates.

He had been hoping Elizabeth might have been able to provide some vital clue to her mother's murder, but unfortunately, nothing of any apparent use was forthcoming. Jarod also figured if she had any valuable information, the police would have already got it from her.

After spending a few more minutes chatting with Elizabeth, Jarod accepted a personal invitation to attend Clarissa's funeral. The ceremony would take place as soon as the investigation was concluded and her body was released from the morgue. Jarod also accepted a hug from the crying woman, then bade his farewell.

~

Late in the afternoon, Jarod got off the tram a few streets from his home. He stopped by the nearby cafe to pick up some more loose herbal tea and some freshly baked pastries. After a quick visit to the second-hand bookstore next door, somewhere Jarod should stop visiting regularly if he wanted to avoid his apartment being completely filled with books, he returned to The Paradiso and walked up the stairs to his apartment. He stopped dead in his tracks when he noticed a note pinned to his front door.

The note was a large piece of white paper covered in what appeared to be red writing. Closer inspection revealed the dripping red ink had the appearance of blood. On the paper, the following message had been inscribed:

"YOU'RE THE ONE I WANT"

In that moment, Jarod felt something. A chilling sensation that rushed through his body like an avalanche. There was only one word to describe the feeling.

Fear.

Chapter 14

PAUL AND BRYCE were busy going over all the evidence and crime scene reports from the Porter murder, comparing every detail to the first crime scene. So far, everything seemed to indicate that both murders were committed by the same assailant.

"The post-mortem reports say both victims were struck in the back of the head with a similar heavy object, most likely a hammer," Bryce said, his eyes never lifting from the paper in his hand, "And judging by the angle of impact, our killer is likely to be approximately 175cm or 5'9 in height."

Paul rose from his seat a dragged over one of the mobile whiteboards. He began writing down everything they knew about their unknown subject, including their approximate height; possibly known to the victims; likely carried a bag or backpack containing the hammer and a change of clothes; knowledge of, or access to the children's book; possibly known to Jarod. Paul qualified that last point with a question mark since it was merely speculation at this point.

The last item on the list did not sit well with Paul at all. Like Jarod himself had already pointed out, he was the only real common denominator in both murder cases. He knew both victims. But since he had rock-solid alibis for both killings, he was clearly not a suspect. But it can't just be a coincidence that he knew both victims. Paul was missing a piece of the puzzle.

Jarod needs to be reinterviewed.

Given the latest developments in the case, it would make sense to reinterview him. Paul briefly considered getting Bryce to do it since he didn't know Jarod as personally as Paul did, and would likely solicit more information out of him by asking more objective questions. But Paul also considered Bryce's interview style to be a little combative. While Jarod was unlikely to be fazed by that, the interview would end up being massively unproductive if Bryce got riled up by Jarod's unusual calmness. Paul would handle the interview himself.

He turned his attention to the children's book. At first glance, it seemed like nothing more than any other reference book designed for young, school-aged children. But someone was twisting its innocent words into something dark and macabre.

Once again, it was difficult to believe that the killer would use the code from the book to construct their ghastly messages unless he was certain the police would be able to decode it. Which made it highly unlikely to be a coincidence that the killer's first victim *just happened* to live next door to a highly talented linguist who owned a copy of the very book needed to decode the killer's bloody message. Since Jarod had all but forgotten about the book, which he hadn't so much as thought about since he was a child, the killer would have had to confirm that Jarod still had a copy of the book.

The killer has been in Jarod's apartment.

The thought sent a cold chill down Paul's spine. This killer was playing a more complicated game than Paul had originally realised. He was manipulating events on a much wider scale, and the idea of that was genuinely creepy.

Who had access to Jarod's apartment? Troy!

"Bryce, we should look a little closer into Troy Merrick. His background, any criminal history, and double-check his alibis."

Bryce looked at Paul speculatively, not understanding how Paul had suddenly jumped to Troy as a suspect.

"He has access to Jarod's apartment. I think the killer must have had access to Jarod's place to confirm he still had a copy of the children's book, otherwise his coded messages were unlikely to ever get translated." Paul clarified, to which Bryce nodded.

"I'll get right on it. When I interviewed him, Merrick didn't strike me as the violent type, but the more we uncover about this killer, the more I suspect this guy likes to hide in plain sight. A lot of the evidence we have so far makes a lot more sense with Merrick as the killer."

"Let's not get ahead of ourselves," Paul said, "He may not be the killer. But the killer almost certainly had access to Jarod's place at some point. We should put together a list of anyone who has had access. People with spare keys, visitors, tradesmen – anyone who could have conceivably been able to get into his apartment for any reason. I'm betting out killer's name will be somewhere on that list."

Paul was just about to propose Bryce reinterview Jarod when his phone started ringing.

"Kincaid," Paul answered stiffly.

"The killer has been at my place." Jarod's normally calm voice sounded almost panicked.

"What? What are you talking about?" Paul sat up straight, the hair on the back of his neck prickling with unease.

"There's a note on my front door with bloody writing on it."

"Where are you now?" Paul said, trying to maintain his calm.

"Outside my apartment door. Should I go inside?"

"No! Go downstairs and wait outside the building. Bryce and I are on our way."

Paul ended the call and stood, pulling on his jacket and grabbing his phone and keys. Bryce did the same, and within moments, the two detectives were dashing out toward the carpark.

"The killer's left a note on Jarod's front door. I'll drive, you call the crime scene boys and get them out there ASAP." Paul said as they exited the lift and sprinted toward Paul's car. Bryce was already on the phone when Paul started the engine and tore out of the station car park.

Minutes later, the two detectives pulled up in front of The Paradiso. Paul was relieved to see Jarod standing by the building's main entry, looking shaken but unharmed.

"Are you okay?" Paul asked, his eyes raking over Jarod's body, trying to reassure himself that the other man was unharmed.

"Yes, just a little unnerved. I'd just got home when I found the note pinned to my front door." Jarod said, sounding calmer than he had on the phone.

"Did you touch the note or the door?" Bryce asked, his phone still planted to his ear.

"No, I left everything as it was and called you guys straight away. I'd only just got back from visiting Elizabeth when I saw it on the door. Oh! That reminds me. You should try to track down her ex-husband. Bill and Clarissa had a falling out. Elizabeth thinks he's living in Dubai, but maybe he's back in Australia." Jarod was rambling, obviously more shaken by the experience than he was letting on.

Bryce went upstairs to secure the scene while Paul remained downstairs with Jarod. A few minutes later, the crime scene techs arrived to start processing everything.

Paul hoped that this latest development would yield some valuable new clues to the identity of their killer. Hopefully, doing something like this in broad daylight meant the killer was becoming complacent. A complacent killer is a sloppy killer, and that might mean they haven't been as meticulous as in previous encounters.

Bryce texted, telling Paul and Jarod to join him upstairs. The two men walked up the stairs to Jarod's apartment to see the crime scene techs fingerprinting the front door and the surrounding area. Bryce had the note in a clear evidence bag.

"I don't think this note is from our killer," Bryce announced when Paul came over to view the latest message.

Paul could see immediately why Bryce had come to this conclusion. Firstly, the note was written in English, rather than Cuneiform symbols. Secondly, the note was written in what appeared to be ink, rather than blood.

"Are you sure?" Jarod asked, sounding almost relieved, but also slightly disbelieving at the same time.

"One of the techs did a luminol swab on the note. It's not blood. Probably some kind of soft tip pen, like a red whiteboard marker. Plus it's in English." Bryce summarised. One of the forensic officers came over to them and took the bagged note away for further testing.

"Why didn't I notice that? I can't believe I made such an obvious error. I apologise for wasting your time." Jarod said blandly.

"No. You did the right thing. You saw something suspicious and you called it in straight away. That was exactly what I wanted you to do." Paul stated emphatically.

"I should have realised immediately that it was different from the killer's messages. I can't believe I missed that it was written in English. I think events of the last few days have left me a little distracted."

Paul hadn't realised the murders had so deeply affected Jarod. It was easy to dismiss his feelings since the man didn't really have them. But if last night proved anything, Jarod wasn't quite as unemotional as he first appeared. He placed his hands on Jarod's shoulders and gave them a light, comforting squeeze.

"Hey, don't worry about it. With everything you've been through lately, it's not surprising you're a little distracted. But regardless of who wrote this note, we'll figure it out. I promise." Paul said.

The crime scene techs finish up and clear them to enter the apartment. Bryce heads downstairs, still talking on the phone, while Paul told Jarod to remain in the corridor while he checked out the apartment.

Paul did a quick check of each of the rooms, making sure to check all the obvious hiding places. Everything checked out. Nothing appeared out of place and there was no evidence the person who pinned the note on the door had gained access to the apartment itself.

"All clear, you can come in now," Paul calls out, and Jarod joins him inside, closing the door behind him,

"Thank you, Paul. I appreciate you coming at such short notice. Can I offer you some coffee?"

Paul observed that Jarod was visibly more relaxed now that he was back inside his apartment. He had sounded almost frantic on the phone, which Paul had been stunned to hear, but Jarod was now back to his usually calm, bland self.

"Actually, I better get back downstairs. Bryce is waiting for me. I'll try and drop by after my shift ends if you like?"

"Certainly. I would like to spend some more time with you."

Paul leaned in and gave him a quick, chaste kiss, then headed out the apartment door. He took the stairs two at a time as he descended to the street level. Bryce was standing by the car, ending his phone call as Paul approached.

"That was the building owner. He had the CCTV system repaired yesterday, so we should have footage of whoever posted the note on Jarod's door. The owner is out of town tonight, but he'll meet us here tomorrow morning to retrieve the footage from the DVR in the basement.

"Excellent. What should we do now?" Paul asked.

"Let's call it a night. If we can't get the footage now and the forensics reports won't be in until tomorrow at least, there's not much more to go on right now. Meet you here tomorrow?" Bryce said with a smirk.

His partner was enjoying this way too much.

"Bright and early," Paul said, smirking back.

"Yeah, that's what I thought. Be careful, mate. Sweet dreams."

Paul tossed Bryce the car keys and watched as his partner drove off into the night.

When Paul made it back upstairs, Jarod answered the door while speaking to someone on the phone.

"No, that's fine. I can be there in an hour. No problem. See you then." Jarod ended the call and turned to Paul, "Sorry about that. That was my neurologist. I've booked in for a functional MRI scan. I want to make sure everything is okay upstairs." He tapped the side of his head.

"Are you feeling pain?" Paul was instantly concerned.

"No, nothing like that. But something strange is going on. In the last day or so, I have started experiencing... flashes... of feelings. Then today, I was so distracted by fear, I completely missed that the note was written in English."

"Hey, I think maybe you're overreacting a little. It's normal to be scared given the current circumstances."

"It's not normal for *me*. That's why I need to get it checked out. I'm sure everything is fine, but I just want to make sure."

Paul could understand that. Considering Jarod had completely adjusted to a life without feelings, it would probably be a little unnerving if suddenly he started having them again.

"Do you want me to come with you?"

"No. You look exhausted. You should get some rest. Why don't you go have a shower and get into bed? I'll be back soon."

Paul couldn't deny his fatigue but still wanted to be there for Jarod. He was sure an MRI scan wasn't going to be fun.

"I promise I'll be fine. Now go to bed. I command you." Jarod said with little authority in his voice.

Paul burst out laughing, "Command me? Well, how can I ignore that? Okay, I'll go and rest. Good luck with your test." he leaned in and gave Jarod a kiss.

Jarod grabbed his bag and keys, then departed, ordering a rideshare on his phone as he closed the door behind him. Paul stood there for a moment, rooted to the floor.

I hope he's okay.

Chapter 15

JAROD WAS NO stranger to MRI scans, but despite having been through them multiple times over the years since the accident, he had never got used to them.

As he lay still and straight on the cold metal table, Jarod was acutely aware of everything around him. The loud, almost deafening, banging noises; the claustrophobic feeling of being confined inside a tight metal tube; The need to remain absolutely motionless, lest the scan be ruined and have to be restarted.

Directly above his head, inside the tube, was a small screen which displayed a series of random images and videos. The 'functional MRI' scan he was currently undergoing was specifically designed to examine his neurological reactions to visual stimuli. As soon as the test began, the screen switched on and started showing various images including a beautiful field of wildflowers, a raging bushfire, children playing hopscotch, brutal images of war, random faces, animals being ill-treated, famous paintings and a plate of rotting food, to name just a few.

After forty-five minutes, the test was complete, and the metal table withdrew itself from the hulking machine, allowing Jarod to sit up. The diagnostic imaging technician who had conducted the scan told Jarod he could get up and return to the waiting room; promising the doctor would call for him soon.

After a short wait in the cold, sterile waiting room, Jarod was escorted to Dr Theodore Svenson's office. The room looked like any Doctor's office. Lots of medical books filled a tall bookcase against one wall. The other walls were adorned with posters showing off the different parts of the human brain.

Behind a cluttered, messy desk, Dr Svenson was examining Jarod's scan results on his laptop. The older man with grey hair and deep laughter lines on his face silently gestured for Jarod to take a seat while he flipped through image after image, data chart after data chart.

"So, what were you doing at the time of the first neurological event?" Dr Svenson asked as he continued to examine the scan results.

"I was getting kissed by a man," Jarod said mildly.

Dr Svenson's looked away from the laptop and directed his view at Jarod, his eyebrows shooting up. Jarod suspected he hadn't been expecting that answer.

"I see..."

"Do you think that's what caused it?"

"I'm sure you're boyfriend is an exceptional kisser," the older man chuckled, "But I don't think he's quite capable of that. How did the kiss make you feel?"

"Well, it was interesting. My heart started beating faster and my breathing increased. I felt tingly all over and it... was nice."

Dr Svenson smiled and returned to the laptop and continued viewing the scan results.

"Well," the doctor said absently, "You've got all sorts of activity happening up there, haven't you?" he chuckled again.

I'm not sure what to make of that comment. Was it meant to be a joke? He did laugh after saying it. Perhaps he's trying to keep me calm because the scan has revealed bad news. Perhaps...

"Relax, Jarod. I can see you thinking from here. It's good news. According to the scan, your brain has apparently begun the process of rewiring itself. You have new neural pathways forming to replace or bypass the damaged ones."

It's really happening? My brain is repairing itself? I figured it wasn't going to happen after all this time...

"Now, this process is slow, and there is no way of predicting just how much cognitive and neural function you will eventually regain, but these scans are very encouraging. Based on the cognitive events you described experiencing over the last few days, I'd say you have definitely started to regain at least part of what you lost. Congratulations."

Yeah, congratulations. Here we go again...

"Um, thanks, Dr Svenson. Is there anything I should do, or keep an eye out for?" Jarod asked blandly.

"Just take things one day at a time. It's not unusual for these cognitive events - these bursts of feelings - to come and go as your new neural pathways take shape. So don't be discouraged if you don't feel the full range of human emotion immediately. The possibility exists that you may only ever be able to experience emotional awareness sporadically. But full recovery is not outside the realm of possibility. A positive attitude will go a long way."

"What caused this to happen?"

"Well, to be honest, I don't really know. No one does. The human cerebral cortex is the most complex biological structure known to exist. It's also one of the most mysterious. Nobody fully understands how the brain works, or how it can spontaneously regenerate damaged tissue or even rewire itself."

Jarod sat silently. He was growing deeply concerned about this turn of events. The fact that he was feeling concerned about anything was a source of concern in itself. He was trying to process everything, but he kept coming back to the same core problem.

Can I really go through this again?

"Jarod, why don't you tell me what's worrying you? From the moment you walked in here, you've looked almost distressed. Tell me what's on your mind."

"Can you stop it? Can you perform an operation to stop the new neural pathways from forming?" Jarod blurted out, his breathing becoming rapid as his heart raced.

"Why would you want to stop it?" the doctor asked, his eyebrows furrowing together. Possibly he was confused.

Jarod's heart continued to beat faster, his breathing erratic, the walls felt like they were closing in on him.

"Because I don't want to change again!" Jarod shrieked. Suddenly, everything calmed down. He caught his breath, and his heartbeat started slowing down to a normal rate.

"I'm sorry," Jarod said quietly. He couldn't explain his outburst or the feelings he had just experienced.

Dr Svenson stood up and walked around the old wooden desk, then sat next to Jarod. He gently grabbed Jarod's wrist and took his pulse.

"Take a few deep breaths. In through the nose and out through the mouth. Everything's going to be fine," the old doctor said calmly and reassuringly, "I'd say you just had a little bit of a panic attack. More evidence of how your brain is repairing itself."

Great. Rub it in, why don't you?

"Why don't you tell me more about 'changing' – what is it that you're afraid of?"

"As you know, after the accident, everything about me changed. I stopped feeling things. My personality altered. My behaviour changed. It was a significant adjustment. It took me a long time to get used to living my life this way. Plus, I had trouble grappling with the philosophical side of things. Am I still 'me'? Am I a different person now? Will I ever be the original 'me' again?" Jarod took another deep breath and tried to maintain his calm.

"I've finally got used to who I am now. I'm living my life and getting things done and everything is going well. Now, you suddenly tell me my brain is repairing itself and I'm changing all over again. Plus, I may not recover everything I've lost, so I might be changing into a third, entirely different person."

Jarod felt shaky all over, but for some reason, talking about what he was feeling was helping to keep himself from panicking again.

"How am I supposed to cope with that? Will I be able to handle living with feelings again? Will it affect my work? Will I still like the man I have recently started seeing? Will he still like me if I change? It's too much. I don't think I can handle it."

Jarod closed his eyes and started rubbing his temples. It was an action he used to perform on himself whenever he was stressed, back in the days when he was affected by stress.

"Well," Dr Svenson said, "I'd say, if you are capable of worrying about your situation, you've gone through significant changes already. No, I can't stop the process of your neural pathways rebuilding themselves. We still don't fully understand how the brain is capable of repairing itself in the first place, much less how to stop it. As for your work, I don't see any neurological changes affecting it. You adapted before, as I'm sure you'll adapt again. And if any man rejects you because you recover from a medical condition, then he is most definitely not a man you should be wasting any of your time on. Now, I think that covers everything, doesn't it?" he said with a slight smirk.

Jarod almost felt like laughing. Dr Svenson was wise, and although he was certain the older man was teasing him ever so slightly, Jarod had to admit his panicked outburst was a bit extreme. He felt better now, no longer shaking or feeling like he had just run a marathon.

He thanked Dr Svenson for his time and promised to make an appointment to see him again in a month's time. They shook hands and Jarod departed. Once outside the hospital, Jarod fished out his phone and ordered a rideshare. The car arrived quickly, and Jarod was grateful the driver wasn't interested in small talk.

As the car slowly made its way through the heavy evening traffic, Jarod was deep in thought. Tomorrow would see Troy's still on leave, and Jarod had little pressing work to attend to. He decided then and there that he would take the day off and visit the State Library. It was one of his favourite places. He could examine some of the rare items in their historical collection, or simply get lost in a good book. Either way, it would be a change of scenery and would give him the chance to relax and unwind after everything that has happened over the last few days.

When he got home, he found Paul fast asleep in his bed. Trying not to wake him, knowing full well the detective never got enough sleep, Jarod quietly disrobed and carefully got into bed. As if unconsciously sensing his presence, Paul immediately pulled Jarod into a comfortable embrace. Jarod's head rested on Paul's broad, naked chest and was quickly lulled into a gentle, restful sleep by the rhythm of the other man's heartbeat.

Chapter 16

DESPITE HAVING ASSURED Jarod that the latest note was not from the killer, Paul knew he couldn't be sure of that. This case was complicated, and it would be foolhardy to make any cut-and-dry assumptions about anything. But he wanted, needed, to make Jarod feel safe. Paul only slept for a few hours, then spent the rest of the night wide awake in bed, going over the evidence in his head and analysing all the possibilities. He ended up leaving for work before Jarod awakened.

The new note could be unrelated to the murder investigation; It could be related, but it wasn't from the killer; It could be some kind of hoax; It could be from the killer, but for some reason, they have changed their M.O.; It could be from the killer, but this new note is some kind of distraction or red herring.

He spent hours going over each of the possibilities in his head, trying to figure out which, if any, of them was correct. Unfortunately, like so much of this case, there wasn't enough evidence so far to confirm or dismiss any of his theories.

Regardless of which theory was right, Paul was becoming increasingly disturbed by how much Jarod appeared to be the epicentre of this investigation. He was the common denominator in both killings, and the sudden appearance of this new note on his door seemed to only reinforce his connection.

Paul didn't believe for a second that Jarod was actively involved, but he was now thoroughly convinced that his new love interest either knew the killer or was somehow connected to them in some way.

~

When Paul arrived at the office that morning, he found Bryce sitting at his desk, shuffling paperwork with a frustrated scowl on his face.

"Good Morning, Sunshine!" Paul emoted with false cheerfulness that was sweeter than sugar.

"Bugger off!" Bryce growled with a gruff voice. It was clear his partner had been sitting at his desk for most of the night and hadn't had a wink of sleep. Paul suddenly felt like a prick for not coming into the office too. Or at the very least, brought some coffee and breakfast in for Bryce.

"You want some coffee?" Paul asked, this time in a less cheery, more serious tone. Bryce grunted, and Paul took that as a 'yes.'

Once the two detectives had managed to get some caffeine into themselves, they were feeling a bit more mentally functional, so they began briefing each other on the latest developments in the case.

"Post Mortem and Forensics reports from the Porter crime scene are in," Bryce began, holding up two file folders jammed with papers, "Long story short: there's nothing new. No DNA. No fingerprints. Cause of death was a combination of blood loss and blunt force trauma to the back of the head with a heavy, blunt object. Most likely a hammer. The kitchen knife found at the scene was from the knife block in the victim's own kitchen, so once again the killer didn't bring the knife with them."

Paul groaned with frustration. He had been hoping they would have scored something new with the latest crime scene. Even the smallest clue could help break the case wide open.

"How did you go with the children's book? Any new leads there?" Paul hoped he didn't sound too hopeful, but at this point, he really wanted a new avenue of enquiry.

"Dead end." Bryce said bluntly, "I contacted the publisher, and they said they've been printing that book almost continuously since the early 1980s. It's freely available from just about every public library, bookshop and primary school classroom. There are millions of copies both here and overseas, and no way to get a list of all the purchases. So it's basically untraceable."

Paul had hoped the book had been rare, or at least uncommon enough that they might be able to create a list of owners and start eliminating names. But with that many copies in circulation, it would be damn near impossible to do that with their department's limited resources.

"Hey, don't look too disappointed. We still have the meeting with the building manager this morning," Bryce reminded him, "We should have some pretty juicy CCTV footage to go over. Hopefully, we'll have the bastard on camera, and we can finally identify them once and for all."

Paul didn't bother going into his theories that the note might not actually be from the killer, mostly because he was sure Bryce had already come to the same conclusion. But Paul held out hope that perhaps this CCTV footage would be the big break they desperately needed, and that this case would soon be wrapped up.

When they arrived at Jarod's building, Kenneth Lasky, the building's owner was waiting for them by the main entrance. The two detectives briefly greeted him, before being escorted downstairs into the basement level.

One side of the basement had been divided up into a series of walk-in storage cages, one for each of the apartments. Paul noted the cage assigned to Jarod's apartment was jam-packed with large boxes, presumably filled with more of his extensive book collection. The other side of the basement featured access to the building's services, such as the electricity and gas meters, cleaning cupboard and a large, solid door marked 'Security Area' which Lasky was unlocking with a key on his quite sizeable set of keys.

Upon opening the door, Lasky led the way into a sophisticated monitoring room. A small desk held a single desktop computer and several banks of backup drives, while the wall behind it was dominated with large flat-screen monitors that displayed camera feeds from in and around the Paradiso building.

"What date were you looking for again? I'll bring up the footage and transfer it to a portable drive." Lasky said as he sat at the desk and began typing at the keyboard. Bryce gave him the relevant time and date information. Lasky typed furiously, and soon one of the monitors began displaying the footage from the previous day.

"There we are," Lasky announced, "That's the feed from outside Apartment #04."

The two detectives watched as a figure emerged from the upper stairwell, slowly approached Jarod's door, then tacked up the note. Paul instructed Lasky to pause the footage, and the image freeze-framed on a clear shot of the figure in profile.

"I know that guy," Bryce said, "We interviewed him after the first murder. That's Jarod's upstairs neighbour." Bryce began flipping through his notebook.

"Barry Rawlings. That's definitely him. Didn't Jarod say something about Rawlings harassing him? Unwelcome advances or something?"

"He did," Paul said, his eyes narrowed on the image on the screen, "Mr Lasky, can you please transfer this footage over to the portable drive? We're going to need it for evidence."

Lasky nodded, then set to work transferring the footage. Minutes later, he handed Paul a portable drive, and the two detectives thanked him for his assistance.

Once upstairs, Paul decided to check on Jarod before going up to speak with Barry Rawlings, however when he knocked there was no answer. A quick exchange of text messages confirmed that Jarod was at the library and would be home later in the afternoon.

They proceeded to the upper level and Bryce knocked on Rawlings' door. No response. Bryce knocked again, but this time a lot less subtly. Paul tried to maintain a neutral expression, but he couldn't help but find it funny how quickly his partner went from polite to battering ram in no time flat.

Eventually, the door opened, and the detectives were confronted by a shirtless, sweaty, foul-smelling Rawlings. They had apparently interrupted him exercising. At least Paul *hoped* that's what they had interrupted. Paul and Bryce flashed their badges and the man appeared to visibly pale.

"Barry Rawlings," Bryce said in his rough, deliberately intimidating voice, "Detectives Gordon and Kincaid. Melbourne City Homicide. We'd like you to accompany us down to the station to assist us with our inquiries."

Paul knew there were two reasons for doing this. Bryce wanted to get this guy off balance, hopefully enough that he will give himself away if he really is the killer. Also, Bryce would do anything to avoid going back into Rawlings' stench pit of an apartment.

"B...But, I haven't done anything wrong!" Rawlings protested, looking panic-stricken and terrified.

"Relax," Paul said, "You aren't under arrest. We just need to ask you some questions. Perhaps you should get dressed and we can go."

Rawlings nodded dumbly, apparently calming at the news that he wasn't actually under arrest, but still visibly nervous. He backed away from the front door and quickly changed into a new outfit. The clean clothes did nothing to cover his omnipresent body odour, and Paul was inwardly cursing Bryce for choosing to do this down the station, given they had driven here in Paul's car. The two detectives escorted Rawlings downstairs, noting with interest how the man stared longingly at Jarod's front door as they passed it.

Chapter 17

WHEN JAROD GOT home that evening, the sun had set and it was well after dinner time. He briefly considered stopping off somewhere on the way home for a bite to eat, but he was tired and ready to call it a night.

His excursion to the State Library had been just what Jarod needed. It had been the perfect diversion to help clear his mind and relax him after what was turning out to be one of the strangest weeks he'd experienced since the accident. The State Library had always been one of Jarod's favourite places to go when he needed to escape from his everyday life and centre himself.

His day had begun with a special, by-appointment visit to the library's archives, where he had the privilege of examining a recently acquired rarity – a handwritten letter by one of Australia's most beloved poets, Banjo Patterson. The curator had supplied Jarod with a pair of anti-static cloth gloves plus a face mask and even allowed him to hold the fragile, yellowed paper briefly. The letter itself was unremarkable; simply a brief note thanking the addressee for their kind invitation to a social engagement that, a century after the letter was written, had now been long forgotten and reclaimed by the mists of time. But the fact it was written by the same hand that wrote *The Man From Snowy River* fascinated Jarod endlessly.

After he visited the archives, Jarod went upstairs to the public areas of the library and spent a pleasant day walking amongst the stacks, perusing their vast collection of books. Jarod selected a few fascinating tomes in the foreign language section, including a rare first edition copy of *The Metamorphosis* by Franz Kafka, written in the original German, and settled himself in one of the library's private reading rooms.

Jarod couldn't help but notice the irony of his choice of reading material. He too was undergoing a metamorphosis, although while

Gregor Samsa transformed into a giant insect, Jarod wasn't entirely sure what he was transforming into.

The day flashed by as Jarod lost himself in a world of words. Before long, one of the library staff was forced to interrupt his escape into fantasy to inform him the library would be closing soon. Jarod dutifully returned the books to their correct shelves and left the building feeling tired but renewed. Although Jarod was certain most people wouldn't find a day of Kafka in a dusty old library to be a rejuvenating experience, it was just the tonic Jarod needed to get himself back to normal.

Whatever 'normal' meant now.

As Jarod slowly walked the now darkening streets towards home, his thoughts turned to his rapidly changing neurology. Before the scans, Jarod had been able to almost dismiss the strange feelings he had begun to experience. But now with confirmation that his brain was rewiring itself, it was difficult to delude himself.

Even sitting in the library, there had been no escape from the changes. The feeling of creeping excitement as the curator slowly and carefully unpacked and unwrapped the Patterson letter. A sense of mild amusement at the absurdity of Kafka's surreal prose as he read *The Metamorphosis*. There was even a slight hint of annoyance at being interrupted by the librarian when it was almost closing time.

There was no denying it anymore. The days of being emotionally vacant were over. This was the reason he had needed to take a day out of his schedule and visit the library. Between murders, threatening notes and unstable neurological events, Jarod was not coping well with the disruption to his normally well-ordered life, and for the first time since the accident, he was beginning to experience anxiety.

He longed for the days of peaceful, emotionless serenity. Working quietly at home. No ups or downs. Just his mild, glacial thoughts and his books to keep him company.

Well, to be fair, he wasn't exactly a bubbling eruption of feelings as yet. But who knew how long it would be before he started having public emotional outbursts? Possibly he would start crying uncontrollably or laugh during inappropriate moments? Perhaps he would never do either of those things. Maybe he would only ever experience partial recovery and would spend his days wondering when the next random mental moment would sneak up on him like a predator in the night.

Jarod shook his head as he reached the main entrance to The Paradiso. He was getting himself worked up over nothing. He attempted to reign in his rising anxiety by telling himself that nothing is set in stone yet, and he would just have to take each day as it came. There's no sense in panicking over things that *might* happen.

Now that's my cold, logical self kicking in!

He made his way up the stairs but stopped in his tracks when he reached the second story landing. He was confronted by the sight and smell of Barry, hanging around outside Jarod's front door. Jarod tried to regain his serenity, but it had been swept away by a rising feeling of frustration that he was having trouble containing. He approached Barry, who was red-faced. Jarod instantly recognised he was furious.

"Did you tell them I killed Clarissa?" Barry said in a low, icy voice.

"What? What are you talking about?"

"I just spent eight hours down the cop shop because of you. Because of that stupid fucking note! What have you been telling them, Jarod? That I'm a killer?"

"*You* sent that note?" Jarod was livid, "I told the police about it because it may have been relevant to their investigation. I had no idea *you* sent it. Why would you do that?" He was quickly losing his calm and wanted nothing more than for Barry to go away so he could go inside and end this day.

"I just wanted you to give me a chance. I'm a nice guy, Jarod. But every time you see me in the hallway, you dash off. You won't give me the time of day. I just want to take you out and show you how good we could be together..."

Jarod was done. He was overtaken by an overwhelming feeling of hostility. His face felt hot and his hands were shaking.

"I don't care, Barry!" He shrieked, "I don't fucking like you! For four years you've been harassing me, begging me to go out with you. I've tried to be polite. I've told you I'm not interested. But you just won't take the hint. Back off and never speak to me again. Never approach me again. And while you're at it, buy some soap and deodorant. You stink! You make everyone in this building want to vomit simply by stepping out of your apartment! Stop being a selfish jerk and start thinking about how your behaviour affects the people around you, you rancid-smelling dickhead!"

Jarod was screaming by the end of his rant. Barry's mouth opened and closed like a fish out of water gasping for breath, so stunned by Jarod's outburst. But Jarod cut him off before he could say anything more.

"No, don't say another word. Just go. If you approach me again in any way, I'll get a restraining order." Jarod said much more calmly.

Barry, seemingly at a loss for words, simply turned away and walked upstairs toward his apartment. When Jarod heard a door slam upstairs, he let out a long breath he didn't realise he had been holding on to.

"Are you okay?" A familiar voice said quietly from behind him. Jarod turned around to see Paul walking up the stairs toward him.

"I don't know what okay is anymore," Jarod said, his voice barely a whisper.

Paul folded Jarod into his big, warm arms and held him for a few moments as he took a few calming, steadying breaths. Eventually, they moved into the apartment, and Jarod sat in his usual chair while Paul went off to make some tea.

"No, wait! I should be doing that!" Jarod protested, but Paul ignored him.

"You just sit and relax. Let me take care of you, sweetheart."

Jarod relented and waited patiently. Paul soon emerged from the kitchen with a steaming mug of Camomile tea. Jarod was feeling much more like his old self again. Calm. No more shaking. Neutral. He took a sip.

"How's your tea?"

"You made it wrong. It's too weak."

Paul frowned.

"I mean, it's lovely, thank you."

Paul continued to frown, but for some reason, he was now smirking slightly at Jarod's awkward attempt to cover his unvarnished words.

"You feeling up to talking about what just happened out there."

"Are you asking as a cop?"

The frown was back.

"I'm sorry. This has been a weird couple of days. I seem to be worse at censoring myself than usual. Between murders and threatening notes and scan results, I might actually be experiencing a little bit of stress."

The frown was gone in an instant, replaced with a face drained of colour. Paul darted across the room and held Jarod's hands.

"Scan results? Is everything okay?"

"Depends on your perspective, I guess. They conducted a functional MRI scan and discovered my brain has begun rewiring itself."

"Well, that's a good thing, isn't it? It means you're getting better?"

"No, I'm not so sure it is a good thing. I've been through this already. After the accident, I had to adapt to an entirely new way of living. A life without feelings or emotions. My personality changed. I quite literally became a new person, because I was no longer the same person I was before the accident..." Jarod wasn't sure how he could explain this to Paul. He wasn't sure he entirely understood it himself. His situation was fairly unique.

"I'm not sure how I'm going to adapt to this," Jarod began, "I don't know how I'll cope. Will I still be me if I change again? Will I be the person I was before the accident? Or will I be someone entirely different again? And what about you? You like me. What if you don't like the new me? What if I suddenly don't like you anymore? It's too much..."

Paul cut him off with a searing kiss, licking at Jarod's lower lip until granted entry. Paul's hands moved up to either side of Jarod's head, holding him in place. Jarod's heart began beating out a samba rhythm as he fell into the exquisite sensation of Paul's passionate affections.

"Let's take this one step at a time, okay? Nothing in life is certain. People change all the time. Yes, not all of them have traumatic brain injuries, but we're all constantly changing and growing as individuals. We change to suit our circumstances. There are no guarantees in anything, but especially in love," Paul's words left Jarod speechless.

"I like you, Jarod. Maybe, even more than like. You're smart, you speak your mind. You're honest and you don't play games. Those things are unlikely to change. Instead of worrying about what *might* happen tomorrow, why not focus on the here and now?"

Jarod leaned back and looked into Paul's eyes. He was making a lot of sense. He was also saying a lot of things that Jarod himself had been telling himself already. Paul was reinforcing everything Jarod believed, which seemed to calm him and make him feel like he was on the right track. Jarod leaned forward and kissed Paul gently.

"Thank you."

"For what?"

"For helping me. For letting me vent. For understanding. For being here with me."

"No worries. I care about you. I know we haven't known each other long, but I just feel this connection with you."

Jarod felt the same. Ever since they first met, he had felt something was different about Paul, but he couldn't identify what it was. Now, sitting here in Paul's arms, he felt safe and cared for. Like this was the place he was meant to be.

"Do you have to go back to work?"

"Not tonight, I don't, sweetheart."

"Will you stay? Will you... make love to me?"

"Are you sure?"

"I'm sure. Who knows what tomorrow will bring? All that matters is here and now."

Paul smiled, then leaned in and kissed him deeply. Before he knew what was happening, Paul had swooped in, picked Jarod up in his mighty arms and was carrying him toward the bedroom.

"My brain may be on the fritz, but I can still walk, you know!"

Paul just laughed, held him closer, then continued carrying him, "I like carrying you."

"Have it your own way, Caveman Copper!" Jarod said with resignation, as he was carefully deposited on his bed. Paul made an exaggerated caveman noise, and Jarod felt his lips curl at the sides ever so slightly.

"Did you just smile?" Paul said, his eyes ablaze with glee.

"No, of course not. You know I don't smile."

"I think you did! I think you just smiled!"

"Preposterous. Must have been your imagination. Or a trick of the light..."

"Oh, I don't think so. I think you smiled. I think you like the whole Caveman Copper thing. I think I might just have to find some other ways to make you smile."

Paul stripped off his shirt and carefully lowered himself over Jarod on the bed. He lay sweet, featherlight kisses up Jarod's neck until he reached his ear. Taking Jarod's earlobe between his teeth, he gently bit down and Jarod felt a jolt of electricity go through him, making him gasp.

"Did that make you smile?" Paul cooed smoothly.

"No, but it felt... amazing."

"Just you wait, sweetheart. I'm going to make you feel more than just amazing."

With that, Paul began carefully relieving Jarod of his clothes, starting with his sweater vest, shirt and belt. Paul kissed and licked each expanse of naked skin as it was revealed, worshipping Jarod inch by inch. By the time they were both naked, Jarod was shaking with anticipation.

"Do you… did you bring supplies?" Jarod asked, suddenly realising he hadn't had the need to buy condoms or lube for a very long time. He needn't have worried. Paul smiled, bent down and retrieved a foil packet and a small sachet from his discarded trousers.

"Always prepared, huh?"

"I'm a detective. I have to be ready for anything." Paul smirked as he set the condom and lube on the nightstand.

"Really? Who would have thought Homicide was such a hotbed!"

"How's this for a hotbed?" Paul challenged as he kissed his way down Jarod's chest, over his stomach and swallowed his now achingly hard cock to the root. The tight, sublime heat of Paul's mouth had Jarod's brain quickly turning to mush. He couldn't think. All he could do was whimper as Paul's talented tongue slowly circled his crown, dragging out the most exquisite pleasure. He could feel his balls starting to pull up, and his release was barrelling upon him.

"Stop, I'm going to…"

Paul released his cock with a pop, "Are you sure? You can come more than once you know?"

"I want us to do it together. Our first time, I want it to be us." Jarod panted.

Paul smiled and kissed Jarod deeply, blindly reaching for the lube and condom. Jarod ran his hands through Paul's thick, scruffy hair, noticing the other man enjoyed the sensation of his fingernails gently rubbing against his scalp. Suddenly, Jarod felt a lubed finger running along his crack and then gently pressing against his hole.

"Don't worry, sweetheart. We're going to take this nice and slow. I'm going to make it good for you. For us."

Jarod lay back and relaxed as Paul lavished his delicate attentions upon his entrance. Once he felt Paul's finger carefully slide inside of him, Jarod gasped at the intrusion but quickly felt the burn and stretch turn to warmth and electricity when Paul crocked his finger ever so slightly and grazed his gland. It was like lightning flowing through his body.

"There it is. There's the sweet spot." Paul murmured as he slid a second finger into Jarod's entrance. Soon, a third was added and Jarod felt stretched out and full. All the while, Paul was gentle and quietly spoke words of encouragement. Jarod had never had a lover give him so much intimate attention. Although, Jarod had never had that many lovers, he was beginning to realise his past experiences had been pretty average compared to Paul's passionate lovemaking skills.

"Are you ready? Or do you want me to prep you some more?" Paul asked, his eyes alight with desire.

"I want to feel you inside me, Paul. I want you to make love to me now."

Without another word, Paul snapped on the condom, lubed himself up, and got into position over Jarod. He carefully lifted Jarod's legs and perched them on his wide, muscular shoulders. Paul lined himself up with Jarod's entrance and carefully pressed forward slightly. Jarod felt as his inner muscles gave way and allowed Paul to slip forward, inch by delicious inch, until he was fully seated.

"Are you okay? I won't move until you're ready."

"I feel stretched out and so full. Your cock is so thick."

"Do you want me to pull out?" Paul's face was a study in concern.

"No, don't. It's easing. I can't believe how big this feels. I need you to move. Please, Paul. Please move!" Jarod was panting again, but this time, he was panting with desperation. He could feel Paul inside him, filling him, pressing against his prostate. The sensation was glorious and maddening. He could feel his own hips moving involuntarily, desperate to feel Paul's cock plunge in deeper.

"Relax, sweetheart. I'll give you what you need."

Paul carefully pulled out slightly, then quickly thrust back in. Jarod's head flew back against the pillow, completely unprepared for the jolt of pure pleasure that just ran through him. He bit his bottom lips, desperate not to scream. Paul thrust again, this time increasing his pace. Jarod brought their lips together and they kissed and Paul started fucking him with a powerful rhythm.

"You're so tight. I can feel you clenching down around me. Fuck, I knew I could make you smile!"

Jarod couldn't help it, he burst out laughing. He hadn't done that in years. Paul was making him feel things he never thought he'd ever feel again. Just then, the deep sensation of Paul shifting his angle and nailing his prostate with every inward thrust made Jarod gasp for breath. All rational thoughts left his head as wave after wave of unbridled delight crashed over him. Paul grasped his cock and began pumping him as he continued to pound into him.

Soon, Jarod could feel his orgasm building again. He couldn't stop it now if he wanted to. He tried to call out to Paul, but Paul was standing at the precipice with him. His thrusts had become erratic as he approached the edge. Moments later, both men crashed over together, Paul stiffening as he filled the condom, Jarod spraying his release over his chest. Paul leaned forward and kissed Jarod gently, smoothing the sweaty strands of hair off his forehead.

Paul pulled out gently, disposed of the condom in the bathroom bin, and returned to the bedroom with a warm washcloth. Jarod was only vaguely aware of Paul cleaning him up. His brain was officially shattered from the most powerful experience of his life. Eventually, he was enveloped in warmth as Paul returned to the bed, pulled him into his arms and the two men drifted off to sleep.

Chapter 18

THE NEXT MORNING, Paul woke up feeling more refreshed and relaxed than he had been in years. Making love with Jarod last night had been one of the most mind-blowing experiences of his life, and only served to reaffirm his belief that the two of them shared a rare and special connection.

Paul wasn't a fool. He understood that their relationship was moving at lightning speed. After all, they had only known each other for a few days. But this was the first relationship he had ever had where everything felt effortless; like all the pieces of the puzzle fell into place naturally without conflict or confusion.

It would be easy to get swept up in the moment, but Paul wasn't going to risk ruining the best thing that had ever happened to him by trying to run before they could walk. He wasn't going to do anything insane like propose marriage or suggest they move in together at this stage, but he certainly wasn't going to let Jarod slip through his fingers. In Jarod, he had found something rare and special. He wasn't going to risk losing him now that he knew that the sweet little guy was his one and only.

When Paul finally opened his eyes and allowed those first beams of morning light wash over him, he immediately noticed two important things. The alarm clock on Jarod's nightstand read 8:07 AM – which meant Paul had massively overslept and was now running late for work – and that Jarod was nowhere to be seen. Paul quickly made use of the ensuite bathroom, then scrambled to put on his discarded clothes from the night before.

Paul was not looking forward to making the inevitable call to his partner. He didn't make a habit of running late for work but sometimes, with Melbourne traffic being a nightmare at the best of times, it was simply unavoidable. Paul knew from experience he would cop an earful from Bryce, who always hated it when he was running late. Paul would have to quickly make a pit stop at his place for a shower and a change of clothes, then head into work. Hopefully, he shouldn't be too late by the time he eventually made it into the station.

When he emerged from the bedroom, he found Jarod sitting on the couch, frowning at his phone.

"Good Morning."

"Hi. Oh! I forgot to wake you. I'm sorry. Are you going to get in trouble with work?"

"Bryce will have a moan at me, but nothing I can't handle. Is everything okay?"

"Troy is running late this morning."

"It must be the day for it," Bryce smirked as he leaned down from behind and kissed Jarod chastely on the cheek.

"No, he should have been here over an hour ago. I've called and texted but he isn't answering..."

Paul couldn't help but notice a hint of anxiety in Jarod's usually calm and even voice. He seemed to be genuinely concerned about his assistant.

"Maybe he's stuck in traffic or maybe he missed his tram?"

Jarod gave him a look that made it clear he was not convinced. Paul tried to lighten the mood.

"Maybe he got lucky last night, too?"

Jarod looked at him blankly, but his lips curled ever so slightly at the edges.

"Yes! Made you smile again!" Paul cheered triumphantly. He raised his arms in exaggerated victory. Although, he had to admit, getting a smile out of Jarod was definitely something worth celebrating.

"Go to work, goofball!" Jarod said, his smile widening, "Go catch me a bad guy."

"Yes, sir!" Paul replied with a mock salute and kissed Jarod's cheek again, "I'll call you later. Maybe we can have dinner?"

"Sounds good. Be careful out there."

"I always am. See ya later, Chuckles."

"Chuckles?!" Jarod sounded almost indignant at his new nickname. Paul just laughed and let himself out of the apartment and headed downstairs to his car.

~

Freshly showered and dressed in clean clothes, Paul was only slightly late for work. When he walked into the Homicide offices, he braced himself for what was to come.

"Well, well, well! Sleeping Beauty has finally decided to join us!"

Paul rolled his eyes and sat down at his desk, as Bryce sat opposite with a smug grin on his face.

"Shut up, mate. Like you've never slept in before."

"Nearly two hours late for work? How highly unprofessional..." Bryce's smirk was almost iridescent.

"As I recall, you were once *four* hours late for work. Wasn't that the night you spent with... oh, what was her name again? Oh, yes! Angie!" Paul was now smirking. Bryce's face froze, the smug smirk erased. But slowly, a self-satisfied grin appeared in its place.

"Yeah, Angie," he said softly, clearly remembering a very enjoyable night.

Paul smiled and knew Bryce would let the subject drop for the time being. But he was smart enough to know he would be copping little digs about his tardiness all day.

"Well, if you've had enough beauty sleep, perhaps you can help me go through these witness statements? See if we missed anything. Otherwise, I'm not sure what else we can do for the moment. We keep hitting dead ends."

"Agreed. Just when I thought we finally had our killer, he turns out to be a desperate creep with a crush. Man, you should have seen Jarod go off at him last night. Full. Blown. Rage. Fit. I almost felt sorry for Barry."

"Jarod? Jarod had a rage fit? I thought he was some kind of robot or something?"

Paul frowned, "That's not funny, mate. He had an MRI scan, and apparently, his brain is started recovering. He's slowly starting to get his feelings back. As Barry sure found out last night."

"So," Bryce said, leaning back in his chair, "The little bookworm is actually a little spitfire! Maybe he'll keep you in line. Although, he'll have to work on waking you up on time in the mornings."

Paul was stunned.

"I'm a detective, nitwit. Did you think I wasn't going to notice the way you were looking at him? Relax, I'm happy for you, man. About time you found yourself a decent bloke."

Paul smiled. He had been concerned Bryce was going to razz him about getting involved with someone related to the case. But Bryce wasn't just Paul's partner. He was his best mate, too. Knowing Bryce approved of his relationship was a massive weight off his shoulders.

And with that, the two detectives began digging through the seemingly endless piles of paperwork that this case was generating. But after an hour or so, they were getting nowhere fast. Paul's phone began ringing in his pocket. He quickly fished it out, saw the Caller ID and smiled.

"Hi, Sweetheart. How's it going?"

"Not good. I still haven't heard from Troy. Paul, I'm really starting to get worried. He's never late like this and he *never* has his phone out of his hand. He should have responded to my texts by now. Something's wrong."

"As I said before, I'm sure he's fine, but we can swing round there later and check on him if you like?"

"I'd appreciate it. You'll call me as soon as you go over there?"

"I promise. Relax. I'm sure Troy just has a hangover or something. I'll call you later." Paul said, trying to sound confident for his lover. He ended the call and looked over at Bryce, who was giving him a puzzled look.

"That was Jarod. His assistant didn't show up for work this morning and he's not answering his texts or calls." Paul explained.

"Let's go over there now and do a welfare check. I want to speak to Troy anyway. I'm still a bit suss about him."

"Didn't all his alibis check out?"

"Yeah, but that doesn't mean he isn't involved. What if he wittingly or unwittingly gave the killer information about the children's book? I'm clutching at straws, I know, but it's all we have to go on right now," Bryce was not even trying to disguise how much this case was frustrating him.

"I also want him to make a complete list of everyone he can think of that's been in Jarod's apartment."

"Jarod already did that for us," Paul said, puzzled.

"Yeah, but Troy might remember someone Jarod forgot. I also want to expand the list to *every* possible person who has been in his apartment – no matter how briefly. Did he get the locks changed when he moved in? If so, who was the locksmith? Has he had a plumber in to fix something? Removalists? Carpet cleaners? Someone who randomly knocked on the door like an Avon Lady or Jehovah's Witnesses? I don't want to exclude anyone, no matter how minor their interactions might be. If Troy isn't involved, then the killer *has* to have had access to the apartment. If we make a complete list, the killer's name will *have* to be on it."

Paul mulled this over. Bryce made a good point. Whether or not Troy was involved, (the possibility of Troy being in league with a killer was utterly far-fetched in his opinion) Bryce was right about making a more complete list of people with access to the apartment.

"Okay. Let's head over there now. Hopefully, Troy's hangover isn't too bad and he can give us some good intel. We need a break in this case badly." Paul said as he grabbed his stuff, put on his jacket and followed his partner to the lifts.

~

As they sped through the busy city streets toward Troy's home, Bryce driving like he was attempting to qualify for the Bathurst 1000, Paul was starting to feel a creeping sense of unease. Jarod wasn't prone to over-reacting to things. If he said Troy being late for work was out of character, then maybe Paul's assumption that Troy was merely hungover was completely unwarranted. The closer they got, the more uneasy he felt. He couldn't seriously imagine Troy, of all people, being involved in this case, but he also couldn't eliminate the possibility either.

They managed to score a parking space directly outside Troy's apartment building, a converted warehouse near the Docklands. Unlike the swanky, expensive apartment buildings surrounding it, Troy's building was cheap, poorly maintained, and its unkempt exterior made it easily mistaken for a condemned structure. The two detectives walked through the unattended ground floor lobby and made their way up the stairs to the top floor.

As they approached Troy's apartment, the first thing Paul noticed was the front door wasn't closed. The heavy hardwood door was hanging slightly ajar, highly unusual for a building like this. Most people wouldn't leave their door open like that unless they wanted to get robbed.

Paul silently signalled for his partner to stop. The two detectives pulled out their sidearms and took up positions on either side of the door. Paul knocked sharply, allowing the door to open a little further. He couldn't see any movement within the apartment.

"Troy? It's Jarod and Bryce. Are you in there?" Paul called out slightly louder than was necessary. He listened carefully, but there was no response. An eerie, unnatural silence was all that emanated from within the dark, still interior of the apartment.

"We have probable cause," Bryce whispered, "Plus we're here on a welfare check."

Paul nodded, and they slowly pushed the door open and made their way inside. The first thing they saw was another bloody message on the living room wall. They quickly secured the small apartment, checking each room. It was when Paul entered the kitchen, the last room to clear, he found Troy. His body lay face up, on the floor in front of the oven. He had been stabbed multiple times. Bryce joined him in the kitchen and his eyes bulged when he saw Troy.

"Shit," he whispered, "The poor kid. I'll call it in." Bryce shook his head, turned and walked out into the living room to call in the crime scene teams.

Paul looked over the scene, and initially, it seemed all too familiar, with blood splattered all over the walls and cabinets. But there was something about this crime scene that didn't seem right. The fact that Troy had only been stabbed a few times, much less than the previous victims, became all the more unusual when Paul looked down at Troy's right hand. He was clutching a bloody knife. In the previous scenes, the murder weapon had been discarded absently by the killer. But in this case, the victim was actually holding the weapon.

Was this a message? Did Troy fight the killer off? Did Troy stab himself? Surely there are easier ways to kill yourself...

The idea of Troy deliberately stabbing himself and staging the scene to look like a murder was preposterous. Unless... he was, in fact, the killer.

Who else but the killer would know how to stage the scene like this? What was his plan? Was he trying to pass himself off as a victim to throw suspicion on someone else? Did he stab himself too much and die before help could arrive?

Paul was reeling at the horrible possibility that the killer they had been hunting had been right there, in front of his nose, the whole damned time. Worse still, if Troy *was* the killer, he had now, intentionally or unintentionally, escaped justice.

Paul looked down at the man's pale, lifeless face. It was then he noticed the tiniest twitch of Troy's right cheek. Paul reached forward and pressed his fingers to Troy's neck.

"Bryce! He's still alive! Get an ambulance out here, now!"

~

Troy was rushed to hospital under police guard. Until they could sort out what was going on, the two detectives didn't want to take any chances. The paramedics said his wounds were superficial, but he had lost a lot of blood. One of the officers guarding Troy called in shortly after the ambulance arrived at the hospital to confirm that Troy was being taken into emergency surgery, but his prognosis was unknown.

Paul called Jarod and informed him about Troy. Although Jarod seemed to be calm about the news, Paul had now known Jarod long enough to notice the subtle shifts in his voice when he was distressed.

"I'll get my stuff together and head down to the hospital now."

"Sweetheart, Troy's under police guard. You won't be able to see him yet. Besides, he's in surgery."

"But he doesn't have any family, Paul. Someone should be there for him if..."

"Don't worry. I'll take you over to the hospital later. There's nothing you can do for him there right now."

"Okay. Will you be home soon?"

Paul couldn't help but smile at that. Jarod's absent reference to his apartment as Paul's 'home' just felt right.

"I'll be there as soon as I can." He ended the call and got back to work.

Paul and Bryce remained at the crime scene for several hours, gathering evidence and trying to piece together what had happened there. Despite a thorough search of Troy's apartment, they were unable to find anything that linked him to the other murders. If Troy was the killer, this would be consistent with his M.O. of not leaving any traces at his crime scenes. But a lack of evidence would also be consistent if Troy were completely innocent.

"Maybe he tried to kill himself, and for some misguided reason, tried to make it look like he had been murdered?" Bryce suggested as he examined the blood splatter pattern on the kitchen cabinets.

"It's possible," Paul replied absently, "But why? He didn't seem depressed or suicidal. And even if he were, why make it look like a murder?"

"Insurance perhaps?" Bryce said, moving over to the living room and examining the new bloody message on the wall.

"I doubt Troy had any expensive life insurance policies. By the look of this place, he isn't exactly flushed with cash. Besides, he doesn't have any family. Who would stand to inherit?"

"Maybe the killer staged it to look like a suicide, then? Throw us off the scent by making Troy look like the killer?"

"That's very possible. In which case, the killer has screwed up royally. It's unlikely the killer intended for Troy to live."

"Lucky we put him under guard then," Bryce said taking a few photos of the message, "We better hope Troy pulls through. Either he's our killer or our only living witness to who the killer really is."

By the time the crime scene teams were almost finished processing the scene, the afternoon had bled away and the evening sky was slowly fading to darkness. Paul and Bryce still needed to conduct interviews with the other residents of the building. There were no interior security cameras installed, and they had been informed that this part of town had not yet been fitted with CCTV cameras. Hopefully, they would find at least one reliable eyewitness, but Paul wasn't confident. People in this part of town tended to keep themselves to themselves, and usually don't want to be seen talking to cops.

"We need to get this new message translated as soon as possible," Bryce said, showing Paul the clear image on his phone.

"If you show it to Jarod, he'll be able to translate it immediately. He has the code memorised."

"I'll just text it through to him then..."

Paul grabbed his partner's wrist. "No. It's not secure. I don't want anyone finding out about the coded messages. If the media get a whiff of it, they'll have a field day. We'll be inundated with fake codes and copycat messages before we know what's happening."

"Fair enough. I'll go and speak to Jarod. You carry on with the interviews. I'll get back here ASAP." Bryce pocketed his phone and strode out the door like a man on a mission.

Paul called over one of the uniforms to accompany him as he conducted the interviews with the building's residents. But something about this crime scene still bothered him. There was something about it that just felt 'off' and he couldn't put his finger on what. Paul had a feeling that he was missing a vital piece of the puzzle.

Chapter 19

JAROD WAS IN a state of shock. Hearing the news that Troy had been attacked by the killer was not something he had anticipated. When Troy had failed to show up for work that morning, Jarod had initially thought his assistant had simply been delayed. A tram strike, a traffic jam, or even a missed bus could all be responsible for his lateness. But when Troy hadn't responded to calls or text messages, that's when Jarod had truly become concerned.

Troy spent more time on his phone than most teenage girls. He was constantly texting, updating social media feeds and exploring gay dating apps. In the time Troy had worked for him, Jarod had never known him to ignore a text message. That's when Jarod started to panic.

That being said, Jarod was more concerned about Troy having had some sort of accident on the way to work. Perhaps he had been hit by a car crossing the street? Maybe there was a tram derailment and he had been taken to the hospital? The last thing he had expected was for Troy to have been stabbed multiple times and left for dead.

After getting off the phone with Paul, Jarod decided he needed to stop distracting himself from the case, and start focusing on it exclusively. There was nothing he could do for Troy at this stage, and there was no way he was going to be able to focus on his work.

Jarod sat down at his desk with a fresh notebook and started writing copious notes about everything he knew about the killer and the case in general. Every theory. Every idea. Every nugget of information he had gleaned so far. Perhaps if he wrote it all out, it would make it easier to digest. Maybe then he would be able to make sense of it all.

As the words flowed out of him onto the stark white paper of the notebook, Jarod felt his racing heart begin to calm. Words had always been a soothing balm to him and, now more than ever, he needed soothing.

He wrote page after page of details notes covering everything from known and suspected details about the killer, to everything he could recall about each of the victims, their lives and what few details he knew of their crime scenes based on what he had been told by Paul and Bryce.

Eventually, he lay down his pen and took a break. He stretched briefly, then headed over to the kitchen to make some tea. If words were his soothing balm, tea was the thing that kept him going while he healed.

As the kettle boiled, Jarod began coming up with a list of questions that needed to be answered. If he could find the answers, he may just be able to discover the identity of the killer.

Did the killer target the victims specifically, or were they victims of opportunity?

If they were specifically targeted, why was the killer attacking Jarod's friends?

Was Jarod a target too?

Was Jarod even connected to the killings, or was it all just a coincidence?

Jarod didn't think for a second that it was a coincidence. There were simply too many connections that led back to Jarod to dismiss. The more Jarod pondered these questions, the more obvious it was that the killer *must* be someone he knew or was at the very least familiar with. Once the tea was brewed, he returned to his desk and started reviewing his notes. So far, he had little to go on when it came to identifying the killer.

The killer had to have had access to his apartment to confirm he still had the children's book, otherwise the coded messages would have likely gone untranslated.

There was apparently no forced entry at any of the crime scenes. The killer had to have personally known each of the victims, or at the very least been familiar enough with them to ensure that each victim would feel safe enough to invite the killer into their home without resistance.

This point stumped Jarod. Clarissa knew Troy, but never met Justin (as far as he knew) as Justin only visited his apartment once. Post-break up, It was unlikely Justin travelled in the same social circles as Clarissa. Troy didn't know Justin because he was hired as Jarod's assistant long after Justin dumped him. The only logical connection between all three victims was Jarod. Since he knew he wasn't the killer, there had to be someone else that all three victims knew. But he couldn't for the life of him figure out who that could be.

Jarod didn't have a huge circle of friends or acquaintances. He had never been much of a social butterfly by any means. His family all lived interstate or overseas. He worked from home, so he rarely had direct interactions with his clients beyond exchanging email messages. His only work colleague was Troy. He had few outside interests. He wasn't a member of any social clubs, nor did he participate in any group activities. So the number of potential acquaintances who could be viable suspects was remarkably low. He wrote a list of everyone he knew and interacted with, then set about crossing out those who had either been killed (or in Troy's case, nearly killed) or had iron-clad alibis. The list of names was very short indeed.

He had to be missing a vital piece of the puzzle. Something that would explain everything and finally reveal the killer's identity. But no matter how much he reviewed his notes, he wasn't getting any closer to a solution.

Jarod was interrupted from his thoughts by a sharp knock on his front door. For a moment, he considered the possibility that the killer had finally shown up for him, but when he saw Bryce's face through the peephole, he relaxed and opened the door.

"Bryce, is it Troy? Has something happened?"

"He's fine. I just got a call from the hospital. He lost a lot of blood, but luckily his wounds were superficial. He's expected to make a full recovery.

"Oh, thank god!" Jarod gasped, then blushed at his unexpected emotional outburst. Relief flooded through Jarod at the news that his friend was going to be alright.

"Wow, you really have started to recover, haven't you? Paul said you were starting to feel things, but I didn't really believe it until just now."

Jarod was surprised that the burly detective had noticed. Was his changing neurology that obvious already? He wasn't sure how he felt about that, but he definitely felt something.

"So, you and Paul," Bryce said carefully, "You two are... getting closer?"

"Yes."

"And you really care about him?"

"Yes. It's kind of new, feeling the way I feel. But I do care about him."

"Good. But just so we're clear – if you hurt him in any way, I'll destroy you," Bryce said with what Jarod presumed was supposed to be an intimidating facial expression. Jarod didn't really notice, he was just so touched that Paul's friend cared enough to threaten him.

"Awww! That's so sweet!" Jarod quickly enveloped Bryce in a big bear hug, stretching his arms, as best he could, around the big man's barrel-like chest. Bryce stiffened at the unexpected contact.

"I knew under that gruff exterior, there was just a big soft teddy bear." Jarod squeezed the man one last time, then released him.

"If you want to live, you'll never say that about me ever again..." Bryce said gruffly, smoothing out his shirt and fidgeting with imaginary lint.

Jarod almost felt a smile coming on. But then something Bryce had said earlier distracted him.

"Wait a minute. His wounds were superficial? What do you mean?" Bryce was momentarily stunned by the sudden change of subject. He shook his head, but then quickly recovered.

"Troy. He wasn't stabbed as much as the previous victims and his wounds were only shallow. He was found with the knife in his hand. We have a working theory that Troy may have stabbed himself. That's why we have him under police guard at the hospital. We don't want him going anywhere until we've had a chance to talk to him."

Jarod didn't know what to say.

Troy stabbed himself? Why would he ever do that?

He wasn't the best at judging other people's moods, but Jarod didn't recall seeing anything in Troy's recent behaviour that led him to believe he was suicidal or thinking of hurting himself.

"That doesn't make sense, Bryce. Why would Troy do that to himself?"

Bryce shrugged, and it was apparent that the big burly cop had shared all he was going to share. Jarod didn't think it would be wise to push him.

"Would you like some tea? The kettle just boiled."

"No, thanks mate. I actually came around to show you something," Bryce pulled out his phone and started tapping at the screen, "It's the latest message from the killer. I was hoping you could translate it for me?"

Bryce passed the phone to Jarod and he began examining the bloody characters. The first thing that hit him was the message was much shorter than the previous messages. It appeared to be only one word.

"It was found written on Troy's living room wall."

"It says 'SPIDER' – I have no idea what that's supposed to mean, though."

"Spider? As in eight legs and spins webs? I don't get it..." Bryce said absently, obviously trying to figure out what this could possibly mean in context.

"Troy is scared stiff of spiders, but I don't think that's in any way relevant. Also, I don't believe for a second that Troy would have stabbed himself. The presence of the bloody message confirms it. Troy knew I was translating some messages for the police, but he never saw any of them, and he wouldn't know the code."

"He'd know it if he was the killer," Bryce said with cold finality.

"True, but didn't he have alibis for the previous murders."

Bryce grumbled to himself, perhaps unhappy that he hadn't thought of that himself.

"I think the killer was interrupted," Bryce eventually supplied, "I think the message is incomplete. Something may have spooked the killer, and he had to leave before he was finished writing the message. That explains why Troy survived and the message is only one word."

Jarod gave this some thought. It's possible that the killer could have been interrupted by something. But looking at the image of the message, something didn't seem right.

"I don't think so," Jarod said, zooming in on the image on Bryce's phone, "Take a look at the size of the symbols. They dominate the wall. If this was just the first word of a longer message, they would be smaller."

Bryce was scowling now. His dark, heavy eyebrows knitted together in consternation as he studied the image on his phone.

"I didn't think of that. Hey, you'd make a pretty decent detective. So, if the killer wasn't interrupted..."

"I don't know," Jarod said as he tried to come up with a theory, "You said Troy's wounds were superficial. Maybe... maybe the killer didn't realise he was still alive. Maybe Troy played dead and the killer stopped stabbing him?"

Bryce considered this, "I guess we won't know for sure until Troy wakes up and tells us what happened. Hopefully, he'll be awake enough tomorrow for us to interview."

"Can I come too when you do the interview. Troy doesn't have any family, and I don't like the idea of him being alone in the hospital."

"Sure, when he wakes up, we'll make sure you can come and visit him. But me and Paul need to interview him first. He's our only survivor, and his eyewitness account could be just what we need to catch this fucker once and for all."

Jarod nodded his agreement. He understood how important this was. He just wanted to make sure Troy had emotional support during his recovery. Although Jarod couldn't help but be surprised that he, of all people, would be the one to be offering it.

"I should be heading back to the scene. We still have several people to interview before the day is done," Bryce said, turning toward the front door and seeing himself out.

"Call me if you hear anything more about Troy!" Jarod called after him as the detective made his way down the stairs.

Reentering his apartment, Jarod locked the door and let out a heavy breath he hadn't realised he was holding onto. He was so relieved that Troy was going to be okay. But he was deeply concerned about the revelation that Troy had either been attacked by the killer or possibly stabbed himself for some unknown reason.

Jarod sat down at his desk and sipped his now cooled tea. This latest development in the case bothered him. It didn't fit the pattern of the other attacks. The victim was less brutally attacked. The victim survived. The coded message was shorter and didn't really match the style of the previous communications from the killer.

The other messages had been personal messages from the killer to either the police or possibly Jarod himself. 'Spider' didn't hold any specific meaning for him, and Bryce didn't seem to know what the message meant either.

Why the change in M.O.? What does the message mean?

Jarod looked around his apartment for inspiration. Anything related to spiders. Something that might explain this latest message. Aside from a can of extra-strength bug spray under the kitchen sink, he couldn't find anything that directly related to spiders. He moved into his bedroom but, again, failed to come up with anything relevant.

When he entered the library room, he scanned the shelves for a book about spiders. Maybe something with 'Spider' in the title. He found a weathered old copy of *Charlotte's Web*, but closer examination didn't reveal anything of importance.

It was then he noticed something dangling from a nearby shelf. Closer inspection revealed it to be a money spider. It had constructed a small web between a shelf and the row of books beneath it. In the centre of the web, a small fly had made the mistake of getting too close to the spider's silken construction and had become ensnared by its sticky filaments. The spider was busy spinning more silk and using it to tightly encapsulate its prey for later consumption.

"Poor little fella," Jarod thought absently to himself, "I guess you never heard that old proverb – *Come into my parlour, said the spider to the fly...*"

Jarod's heart stopped. In a moment of clarity, it was suddenly and horrifyingly clear. The meaning of the killer's message slammed into him like an unforgiving freight train. Jarod turned on his heel and ran as fast as he could out of the apartment.

IT'S A TRAP.

"Bryce!" Jarod yelled as he jumped the stairs three at a time, desperate to get to the detective before it was too late. Jarod didn't have Bryce's phone number, so all he could do was run.

"Stop, Bryce!" he continued to yell as he burst through the main entry doors on the ground floor. He looked both ways, hoping to spot the detective or at least his car. Down the road slightly, toward the next intersection, he saw Bryce face-down on the road. He was laying next to his car, a shadowy figure knelt by his side, looming over him. The figure was dressed in dark clothes and was facing away from Jarod, so he couldn't make out anything identifying about them. They held what appeared to be a large, heavy hammer, which glistened in the twilight with what Jarod presumed was Bryce's blood. The figure lifted the hammer aloft, their intention clear.

"Stop! Leave him alone! I've called the police!" Jarod screamed as he ran toward them, hoping to scare away Bryce's attacker. The figure turned around, a hooded black sweatshirt projected darkness across their face, perfectly concealing their identity. They froze in place, briefly stunned by Jarod's approach, but they appeared to quickly recover. The figure turned and ran across the road like a terrified rabbit, dashing into a nearby alley and melted away into the evening shadows, their rapid footsteps fading as they made their escape. Jarod fell to his knees by Bryce's side.

"Oh, God Almighty. Bryce! Can you hear me?" Jarod gently shook the detective's shoulder. The detective groaned for a moment before falling silent, giving no further indication of consciousness. The back of Bryce's head was a mass of matted hair, blood and torn skin. Jarod quickly fumbled in the big man's pocket and retrieved his phone. He quickly dialled and pressed the phone to his ear.

"Yes, I need an ambulance. I have an Officer down..."

Chapter 20

THE HARSH, BRIGHT neon lights of the Emergency Department's waiting area only served to heighten the surreal, otherworldly daze that Paul and Jarod found themselves in as they waited for news on Bryce.

Jarod had gone with Bryce in the ambulance and was sitting in the ER waiting room when Paul arrived. Paul had never driven so fast in his entire life after receiving the call from dispatch, notifying him that his partner had been attacked and was en route to the hospital.

Paul, not wanting to focus too much on how he was feeling, decided to spend his time productively. He took Jarod's statement and asked him exactly what happened. As Jarod coldly recounted everything, starting with Bryce's visit, Jarod's realisation that the latest message was a trap, and eventually scaring away the killer, Paul made copious notes. He knew that now they finally had an eyewitness who had actually seen the killer up close, this could be the break they had been waiting for. However, he was disappointed to hear that Jarod didn't get a good enough look at the killer to be able to identify them to any degree of certainty.

Bryce's theory that Troy was involved appeared to have been thoroughly disproven, given that Troy was unconscious in hospital, and under police guard, at the time of Bryce's attack. Whoever the killer was, they clearly knew them well or was capable of anticipating their actions to a surprisingly high degree. The 'SPIDER' trap showed the killer knew at least one of the detectives would immediately consult with Jarod in person, allowing them to lay in wait.

The killer had apparently changed their M.O. once again. This time, they were employing a pattern of misdirection in their attacks. First, making Troy's attack look self-inflicted while simultaneously making Troy look like he was possibly involved in the other killings. Now, the killer had successfully manipulated a police officer into an ambush, which Paul could see was plainly engineered to make Jarod look like he was involved.

Why did everything link back to Jarod? What was the connection?

After taking Jarod's statement, there was little else to do but wait until someone gave them an update on Bryce's condition. The two men sat silently, Jarod's hand soothingly atop Paul's. He had quickly started to fall for Jarod. The man was smart, funny (in his own, dry, slightly off-beat kind of way) and cute as a button. He was also willing to go out of his way to help out in this investigation when other people would have run for the hills – which, in Paul's mind, spoke volumes about Jarod's character.

Although he had only known Jarod for a very short amount of time, he could see a future with him. Deepening their relationship, falling in love, building a life together. He'd been here before, or at least he thought had been. But this time, something just felt different. It felt right. They clicked in a way he had not experienced in any of his previous relationships. Like Paul had found the other half of himself, a half he hadn't realised was missing. When this case was finally over, Paul intended to fully explore these feelings and find out if he and Jarod could really make a go of it.

Paul was shaken from his thoughts when a doctor in scrubs came through the large swinging doors at the other end of the waiting room. His face mask was dangling around his neck and the older man looked exhausted.

"Is there anyone here waiting for Bryce Gordon?" The doctor announced to the room. Jarod looked up and his eyes widened, clearly recognising the man.

"Dr Svenson," Jarod called out as he got to his feet and walked over to meet him, Paul following in his wake.

"Jarod? What are you doing here?"

"I'm a friend of Bryce's"

"I'm Detective Paul Kincaid. Melbourne City Homicide," Paul flashed his badge, "Detective Gordon is my partner."

Svenson pondered this for a moment, "Does Detective Gordon have any relatives here?"

"No. I've left a message to be relayed to his brother. He's currently stationed on a gas rig in the Torres Strait. But it could take days for him to get here."

"Very well. Detective Bryce's condition is critical but stable. He sustained a serious blunt force trauma to the back of his head. It's a miracle his skull didn't fracture, but the force of the impact has caused some brain swelling. I've been forced to put him into a medically induced coma to preserve his higher brain functions and give his brain a rest while it heals."

Paul wasn't sure what to make of that. Brain swelling can't be good. *Did that mean Bryce had suffered brain damage? Was he likely to recover? Was he going to die?*

"How long will he need to be kept in the coma?" Jarod asked.

"At least 72 hours. Possibly longer. If the brain swelling doesn't start to reduce soon, we may be forced to remove the back section of his skull to give his brain room to expand outside of his cranial cavity. Hopefully, it doesn't come to that."

"Is he going to die?" Paul said, barely able to form the words.

"We're doing everything we can for him. He's strong and healthy, plus the impact itself could have been a lot worse. The odds are in his favour."

"Can we see him?" Jarod said, Paul still trying to process everything.

"Give us half an hour. We're setting him up in ICU now. We'll be able to closely monitor his condition there and ensure he gets the treatment he needs. A nurse will come down to collect you shortly."

"Thanks, Dr Svenson. I know he's in good hands." Jarod said, and the doctor turned and walked back through the double doors.

"You know that guy?" Paul asked.

"He saved my life, Paul. Dr Svenson is my Neurologist. Bryce couldn't have a better doctor to get him through this."

Paul was flooded with relief. His initial shock at the news that Bryce was now in a coma had passed, and he was starting to feel positive that his partner would make a full recovery.

A short time later, a young male nurse in crisp white scrubs introduced himself as Max and escorted them upstairs to the Intensive Care Unit. Before entering the unit itself, Max briefed them on the importance of sanitising their hands before they could go in.

"Also," Max said, as the two men thoroughly washed and dried their hands at a nearby wash basin, "Dr Svenson briefed you on Mr Gordon's brain swelling?"

Both men nodded.

"Well, in the event we need to get him into an operating theatre to relieve the pressure on his brain, we have already prepped him for surgery. As a result, we have shaved both his head and face. Mr Gordon has also sustained some bruising and contusions to his face. I wanted to prepare you for that before you went in, so you know what to expect when you see him."

Paul thanked Max for his considerate help, but nothing could prepare him for the sight he beheld when he walked into the ICU and saw his partner lying motionless on the bed. The big, burly detective seemed so much smaller than normal. He had sensors attached to his chest, head and fingers. Machines surrounded the head of the bed, giving live readouts of his vital signs. A breathing tube had been inserted in his mouth to ensure he was getting enough oxygen. Bryce's face was indeed badly bruised and, without all the dark hair, the man was almost unrecognisable. An audible gasp escaped Paul's lips, but he held himself in check and stepped forward to hold his best friend's hand.

"Hey mate. How are you doing?" Paul said in a hushed tone, not wanting to disturb any of the other patients, "I see you found another way to get out of an honest day's work."

Jarod tried to hold back a giggle at Paul's teasing. He couldn't resist giving his best mate a bit of stick. He knew that coma patients could sometimes hear the people around them, so hopefully, Bryce would hear him and wake up sooner. If only to tease Paul back.

"You just focus on getting well. I'm gonna catch this fucker, if it's the last thing I do. I'm gonna find him, and you're gonna wake up, and we're both gonna watch as he gets locked up for life. So, get better soon, mate."

Paul gave Bryce's hand a firm squeeze, took one last look at his mate's bruised face, then stepped away.

Outside the ICU, the two men took a moment to breathe. Despite Max's careful briefing, neither man had truly been prepared to see Bryce in that condition. After a few moments, two uniforms showed up to stand guard over their fallen brother in arms. Reassured that Bryce was safe, the two men made their way downstairs toward the car park.

"Let's go home and get some rest. You must be exhausted." Jarod said, resting his hand gently on Paul's arm when they reached the car.

"I can't. I'm dead on my feet but I still need to report in to my boss. The station is going to be a powder keg. A cop has been attacked. Every cop in the city is going to be out in force to get this prick," Paul said as he unlocked the car and they both climbed inside, "I'll quickly run you home first, though."

"I understand, but you really do need to rest. He and Troy are under guard. I've given you my statement. Do what you have to do, but promise me you'll come home to my place when you're done."

"I promise. I may be a few hours though. Will you still be awake?"

Jarod reached into his pocket and retrieved his keys. He selected one and carefully removed it from the keyring, then handed it to Paul.

"Here's my spare key. Just let yourself in when you arrive."

Paul gave him a quick, chaste kiss in thanks. He wasn't sure if Jarod was aware of it or not, but this little sign of trust meant the world to him. It was yet another sign that perhaps they really did have a future together.

~

After dropping Jarod off at the Paradiso, Paul headed back to the station. As he suspected, every officer there was in a state of fury over the attack on Bryce. Paul did his best to try and keep everyone from going off half-cocked, but he knew that if they didn't find the killer soon, the situation was going to deteriorate rapidly.

Paul had only been in the group briefing for about an hour when his phone rang. Apologising to his boss, he looked at the caller ID and saw it was Jarod. Answering immediately, Paul was surprised that there was no immediate response. Just an odd rustling noise. He was about to hang up when he suddenly heard a muffled voice. It sounded like Jarod, but the voice was soft, almost as if he wasn't close to the phone.

Had Jarod accidentally butt-dialled him?

"You don't need to wear that hoody for my benefit. I know who you are..." Jarod's faraway voice declared.

Paul's heart froze.

Jarod was with the killer.

Chapter 21

JAROD WATCHED FROM the entry foyer of the Paradiso as Paul drove away into the night. He was about to climb the stairs to his apartment when his stomach growled loudly. With all the commotion today, he hadn't had a chance to eat anything substantial. Despite being fatigued, he turned on his heel and headed back outside.

A short walk down the road and Jarod found himself at the Imperial Dragon. He briefly considered getting a meal to go, but since Paul wasn't likely to be back for hours, Jarod decided to eat at the restaurant.

The manager greeted him at the door and escorted him to his usual table, the one near the lobster tanks. Jarod had never ordered a live lobster, but he liked to watch the strange aquatic creatures while he waited for his meal. Ordering the house speciality – Rainbow Steak – and an order of Special Fried Rice, Jarod made himself comfortable with a cup of green tea and watched the crustaceans as they slowly moved about their mirky green tank.

Jarod thought about supplying Paul with his spare key, knowing that such an act can often be a symbolic gesture of intimacy and progression of a relationship. Although they had only known each other briefly, Jarod couldn't help but feel that despite the fact they were two very different people with very different viewpoints, their differences somehow complimented each other nicely. They connected so perfectly and they made a good fit. Paul had seemed happy to receive the spare key, and not just for the sake of convenience. Perhaps Paul felt the same way? That their relationship had been swift, but somehow correct?

For some reason, Jarod's mind kept fixating on the spare key. He knew it was an important milestone in any romantic relationship, but he couldn't help but feel that he was missing something else that was important. There was a reason the key was resonating with him, but a combination of exhaustion and hunger wasn't helping his brain to make the connection.

After enjoying his meal and ordering some extra fried rice to take home for Paul, Jarod made his way back home. As he stepped into his apartment, he thought about how Paul would soon be there. Jarod smiled to himself.

It had been a long time since he had been capable of even experiencing happiness, but to know that those feelings were slowly resurfacing like someone had pulled a breaker and all his long-dormant systems were finally coming back online, Jarod in that moment felt the most content he had ever been in his whole life.

Depositing the fried rice in the microwave for later reheating, Jarod switched on the kettle and set about making a cup of camomile tea. Once brewed, he took his mug over to work desk and sipped it slowly as he stood by the window and looked out at the twinkling city lights.

The spare key came to mind again, and Jarod tried to figure out why it was gnawing at him. What was it's significance? It was just a key. Nothing fancy or important about it. In fact, aside from his sister, the only person who had ever used it was Troy – until Jarod went out and got him his own copy.

The various puzzle pieces appeared in his mind. The fact the killer had to have had access to the apartment. The book. The key. The coded messages. The fact that the victims all seemed to have a direct connection to Jarod.

It hit him like a bolt of lightning. The sudden insight as the final pieces of the puzzle fell into place. The clues clicked together in his head and the answer suddenly came to him. When it was all laid out before him, it was beyond obvious, but he had been too close to see it.

Jarod had made a fatal mistake. He had eliminated someone from his list of suspects that he shouldn't have. Feeling altogether foolish, Jarod couldn't understand how he hadn't figured it out sooner. If he had, so much suffering could have been avoided. He slipped his hand into his pocket and retrieved his ancient phone. Pressing and holding the '4' key, it speed dialled Paul's number.

It was then he felt a cold chill go down his spine. All the hairs on the back of Jarod's neck stood on end, and he was immediately aware that he was not alone in the apartment. Carefully, he pushed the still dialling phone back into his trouser pocket and turned around. A hooded figure was standing on the far side of the living room, a knife in their hand, glittered in the darkness. Jarod recognised it as one from the knife block in his kitchen.

"You don't need to wear that hoody for my benefit. I know who you are." Jarod said calmly. Despite realising he was about to die, he didn't feel an ounce of emotion in that moment.

The figure did not attempt to move. They just stood there, watching impassively.

"Come on, did you really think I wasn't going to figure it out, Caroline?"

The shadowy figure slowly raised their hand and carefully pulled back the hood, revealing the face of Jarod's sister. Her hair, which was normally a cascade of long, flowing brown curls, had been cut back into a severe crew cut. Her face was tired like she hadn't slept in days, but her eyes shone brightly as if she were amused by something.

"Just out of curiosity," Caroline said softly, "How *did* you figure out it was me?"

"Process of elimination. Since the killer had to have had access to my apartment at some point, and there were no signs of forced entry, the killer had to have had a key. The owner has an alibi. Troy was in the hospital when Bryce was attacked. That left only one possibility."

"My brother, the eternal clever clogs. You were always far to smart for your own good. Making me look stupid by comparison. Even when we were kids, you were always showing me up with how smart you were. I guess it's not a surprise that you managed to solve yet another puzzle..."

"Why, Caroline? Why did you do this?" Jarod cut off her rambling, desperate to know what could possibly have motivated her actions.

"I did it for you..." she said with a look of puzzlement on her face, as if she couldn't believe Jarod hadn't worked this out, "You need help, but you're so damned stubborn. You won't accept my help, even when you so obviously need it!"

Jarod couldn't comprehend what he was hearing. His own sister had brutally murdered two innocent people, attempted to murder two more, and was now trying to use him as a justification for her actions. He was filled with anger and hostility, which made his altercation with Barry seem like a minor disagreement.

"You've killed two people! Two others are in hospital and could still die! How could that possibly help me?" Jarod was outraged, his voice betraying his feelings. Caroline looked shocked at his outburst.

"Clarissa was a very old woman. It's not like she had much time left! If killing one little old lady could convince you that you were living in a dangerous neighbourhood and make you move back to Sydney with me, it would be all worth it and you could finally get the treatment you need."

"If anyone needs treatment, it's you, Caroline!" Jarod shouted, "What the hell is wrong with you? Have you completely lost your mind? You murdered my friend so you could take me to more pointless hippy faith healers?"

Caroline laughed humourlessly as if she were galled by Jarod's lack of gratitude. She shook her head and took a step toward Jarod.

"Justin was the one who lost his mind. After killing Clarissa failed to get you to see reason, I asked him to come over here and talk to you. Convince you that going back to Sydney was the best course of action. All he had to do was stick to the plan and it would have worked. But no, he had to go off-script. Coming in here, screaming and carrying on. Worthless little bitch! So, I didn't really have much of a choice. I couldn't risk him telling anyone I was in town, so..." Caroline lifted the knife and dramatically mimed cutting her own throat while making a horrible 'throat-cutting' noise. Jarod's stomach turned.

"What about Troy and Bryce? Why attack them?" Jarod could barely speak. He wasn't sure he wanted to hear anymore.

"I never wanted to kill Troy," Clarissa said matter-of-factly, "He was just a distraction. I wanted to lure that cop boyfriend over here so I could get him out of the way. Once I realised the two of you were seeing each other, I finally worked out what was tying you to Melbourne. If I could get rid of him, I could finally convince you to come home with me. But, then the wrong cop showed up, cocking everything up. Lucky for lover boy, I guess…"

Jarod was in shock. All this death. All this suffering. It was all his fault. He couldn't wrap his mind around it.

"Don't you understand, Caroline. I'm already getting better. Just this week, I had a scan that showed my brain has begun rewiring itself. I'm starting to feel things again…"

"You're welcome, baby brother," Caroline said with cold dispassion.

"NO! No way! You don't get to take credit for that. You don't get to murder people, then claim it was all for the greater good. My recovery has absolutely nothing to do with you. I don't know why you are so obsessed with me getting better, but this has to stop."

"You're my brother. Of course, I care about you getting better," she said as if it were obvious. In that moment, she seemed so innocent and gentle, but Jarod wasn't buying it. This was the same routine Caroline would use with their parents when she wasn't getting her way.

"If you truly cared about me, you would never have done any of this. This isn't caring. This isn't love. It's disgusting, evil behaviour, and I want no part of it. And I don't want anything to do with you ever again. You are no sister of mine."

The finality of Jarod's words seemed to hit Caroline like a wrecking ball. The innocent gentleness was wiped away in a heartbeat, replaced with white-hot fury. She shrieked as she raised the knife and dashed across the room toward Jarod. He quickly sidestepped, causing his sister to miscue and over-balance into one of the massive bookcases.

Jarod tried to get to the front door, but Caroline quickly recovered and blocked his way. She thrust the knife at him but missed. Jarod grabbed the lamp of the end table and hurled it at his sister. She dropped the knife as she deflected the glass lampshade.

Caroline, her face red with unimaginable rage, ploughed forward and grappled with her brother. She forced him into another of the bookcases with a thunderous force. Jarod heard a loud snap and felt a searing pain shoot up his right arm. He used his left hand to swing a punch, connecting with his sister's eye. She screamed, falling backwards onto the wooden coffee table, shattering it into splintered fragments.

Jarod slid down the bookcase, the pain in his arm excruciating. He looked down to see his forearm was at an odd angle. But he didn't have much time to think about it, as Caroline was now back on her feet, having recovered her knife and was looming over him.

A loud bang shuddered through the apartment, and both Jarod and Caroline turned to see the front door kicked in by Paul and what appeared to be the entire Melbourne Homicide Department.

"Police! Drop the weapon!" Paul bellowed, his gun pointed directly at Caroline. Jarod was frozen, unable to move or speak.

"I mean it. Drop the knife or I'll fire!" Paul said again, this time taking aim and readying himself to pull the trigger. Caroline shrieked and made a lunge for Paul, but he squeezed the trigger. The bullet hit Caroline in the shoulder, causing her to drop the knife and hit the ground like a bag of rocks. She was screaming and crying as the other officers moved in, cuffed her and dragged her away as her rights were read to her.

Paul secured his sidearm, then dashed across the room to Jarod, getting down on his knees in front of him and raking his eyes over every inch of him.

"Are you okay? Did she hurt you?"

"I think I need medical attention. My arm..."

Paul looked down and saw the broken limb, then called out to one of the other officers to bring the paramedics up.

"It's okay, sweetheart. It looks like a simple break. Nothing to worry about. It's all over now."

With these words, it felt like a barrier inside Jarod burst, and he could feel his face become wet with tears. He was sad but relieved all at the same time. It was confusing, but it felt good as well, as he let go for a moment while Paul held him comfortingly in his arms.

"Shhh, it's okay. I'm here. It's all going to be alright." Paul quietly cooed in his ear.

"My sister is a serial killer..." Jarod could barely get the words out over his silent sobs.

"Don't worry. We'll get through this together, I promise."

Epilogue

6 months later...

"IS THIS THE last of the boxes?" Paul asked as he looked around Jarod's now almost completely empty apartment. After months of house hunting, Paul and Jarod had finally found the perfect house in a nice, quiet neighbourhood. The contractors had just finished with some minor renovations, and the house was now ready for them to move in to.

The two men had been living together in Jarod's apartment for several months at this point, but the place was clearly way too small for two people, especially with Jarod's extensive book collection taking up so much space. They had spent over a week packing the staggering assemblage of books, and now they were finally ready to transport the last of them to the new house.

"I think so..." Jarod replied absently when he emerged from his former library room, armed with yet another huge box of books. Paul suppressed an eye roll, then relieved his lover of the heavy box.

"Okay, let's get these loaded into the truck before you find any more," Paul said with a smile.

"Love me, love my books," Jarod smirked.

"Well, it's a tough bargain, but I think I can make it work."

Jarod leaned in and gave Paul a quick kiss, picked up another box off the ground then looked around the now vacant apartment he had lived in for so many years.

"Are you okay?"

"Sure," Jarod said, his eyes looking slightly misty, "I just never thought this day would come."

"Don't worry, sweetheart. We're going to create so many new memories at our new house. Plus, your new library is going to keep you very busy."

Jarod smiled at that thought. Paul was always happy to see his lover smile. Despite his progressing neurological recovery, smiling and laughing were still rare events for Jarod. So when they did happen, they were a sight to behold. Paul opened the apartment door for Jarod, allowing him to head out first, then closed and locked the door behind them. Their future lay ahead of them.

~

When they arrived at the new house, Troy was already hard at work unloading yet more boxes from his car. Since finishing up at the university a few weeks earlier, Troy had decided to work as Jarod's full-time translation assistant. Troy would also be living with them in the self-contained granny flat in their backyard, at least until he found a suitable place of his own. His emotional recovery after the attack has been slow going, and Troy couldn't face returning to his apartment. The horrible memories that his home now held were too much for him to bear.

"Hey, guys!" Troy said excitedly as they approached, "It seems we've already made a good impression on the neighbourhood. Our new neighbours have invited us over for a barbecue tonight if we're up for it."

Paul had already anticipated this since it was *his* friends (and now neighbours) Alex and Nick, who had told him about this house when it had first come onto the market.

Paul had first met Alex and Nick a year or so earlier when he was investigating who had been stalking and harassing Alex. The three of them had started hanging out after the case was over and since had become good friends.

He hadn't initially been sure if he and Jarod could afford a house in such an expensive area, but between the sale of his house, Jarod's income and investments, and the fact the house was a bit of a rough diamond in desperate need of some serious polishing, they were able to snag it for a bargain price.

"Well, that's excellent news!" Paul said, "We won't have to worry about cooking tonight. Plus, if Alex and Nick have anything to say about it, we'll be ending the day with a gourmet feast. I hope we can find and unpack the wine. I don't want to show up empty-handed."

Jarod smirked and pulled out a bottle of red wine from his ever-present messenger bag. He had been anticipating a dinner invite too.

~

JAROD HAD SPENT years fantasising about buying his own home, but the reality of stepping into the new house with the man he loved made all his fantasies pale in comparison. The contractors had finished with the major repairs, like the installation of a new kitchen, bathroom and entertainment deck out the back, but the rest of the house still needed a little TLC here and there. A bit of painting and some new carpet upstairs was all that was left to be done. Despite these minor imperfections, the house was exactly what Jarod had always dreamed of.

Stepping through the front door felt like the beginning of a brand new life. After the last few months, Jarod could use a change of scenery. His sister's trial had been mercifully short but was still intensely stressful. Caroline had initially tried to plead not guilty by reason of temporary insanity, but when the phone recording of her confession was played in court, she knew she didn't have a hope of winning and quickly changed her plea to guilty.

While the doctors had diagnosed Caroline with a laundry list of mental issues, she was not only ruled as sane and fit enough to stand trial, but also sane and capable of telling right from wrong at the time of committing her crimes. Once sentenced, Jarod only visited his sister in prison once. Caroline had made it very clear that she blamed him for her arrest and eventual incarceration, and that she wanted nothing further to do with him. Jarod had hoped to salvage some form of relationship with his only sibling, but her intense narcissism would never allow her to accept responsibility for her own actions. Until she could, a relationship with Jarod would not be on the cards.

Jarod had been left devastated and conflicted in the wake of the trial. He was sad to have lost his sister. He was angry about the horrible things that Caroline had done in his name. He missed having his sister in his life. He was sympathetic that she had been mentally ill for so long without treatment, but he also understood that Caroline had known exactly what she was doing when she went on her horrific murder spree.

It would take a long time for Jarod to find it in himself to forgive Caroline for everything that she had done. Forgiveness didn't mean absolution or a willingness to forget her crimes. Forgiveness, in Jarod's mind, was less about making Caroline feel better and more about letting go of the negative feelings that he carried with him as a result of his sister's actions. All in all, his feelings regarding his sister were complicated and difficult to explain. Which, considering his complicated neurological status, went to show just how much progress he was making in his recovery.

Once all the boxes were unpacked from the truck and their cars, Jarod set to work cleaning and setting up the kitchen while Paul and Troy worked on shifting the boxes of books downstairs. It would take a long time to set up the library to his liking, but since the contractors had converted the entire basement level into a combined library and office space for Jarod's translation business, there was guaranteed to be plenty of room for his endlessly expanding book collection.

After setting up the bathrooms and the main bedroom, Jarod came downstairs to the living room to take a short break and was immediately confronted by the sensuous vision of a shirtless, sweaty Paul manhandling their new flatpack wardrobe together. His taught muscles stretched and flexed under his tanned, lightly moistened skin. His rough growling grunts as he banged the nails in was a breathtaking study in masculinity. Jarod needed a cold drink, or perhaps a cold shower, but he didn't want to miss a moment of the show.

"Are you going to stand there all day staring, or are you going to help me with this thing?" Paul said with a sexy smirk.

"I was just admiring the view, and kind of wishing I was that wardrobe right now."

Paul raised his eyebrows in shock. Then he smirked and gave the wardrobe another short, sharp bang with his hammer, waggling his eyebrows, which made Jarod yelp, then giggle.

"I was about to get a cold drink. Why don't you take a break and join me?"

"Sounds like an offer I can't refuse," Paul dropped the hammer on the floor and followed Jarod out to the kitchen where they helped themselves to cans of icy cold soda. The two men headed outside to the entertainment deck to take advantage of the cool afternoon breeze.

Troy had set up all the outdoor furniture on the deck and was now busying himself setting up his granny flat at the back of the garden, with the assistance of a patient Bryce.

Bryce had managed to recover from his injuries without the need for further surgery, but his convalescence had taken quite some time. He had only just recently returned to work, as he had been suffering from periodic migraines and dizziness which prevented him from driving or passing a firearms clearance. But with help from Dr Svenson, Bryce had finally managed to get back to doing what he did best – grumbling and catching bad guys.

Bryce and Troy had quickly forged a surprisingly strong friendship after sharing a hospital room during their recovery. Although, their friendship appeared to be entirely based upon their mutual love of winding the other up. It started when Bryce had given Troy the nickname 'Princess Toadstool' – a nickname that Troy detested. Troy had retaliated by frequently suggesting that Bryce was 'on the turn' by pointing out random pieces of the detective's clothing and claiming that they made him 'look a bit queer.' It started with shorts, t-shirts and even a pair of sneakers. The running gag reached epic heights of lunacy when Troy one day suggested Bryce's perfectly normal black business socks looked a little flamboyant.

"Only gay men wear those kinds of socks," Troy had said with a remarkably straight face.

"Bullshit!" Bryce had spluttered, "They're just socks!"

"Look around, honey!"

Bryce immediately surveyed the hospital room and, to his alarm, noticed that Troy, Paul and Jarod were all wearing the exact same foot garments. Bryce immediately removed his socks and swore he would remain barefoot until someone brought him some of his football socks from home, all the while grumbling about wanting to transfer to a different hospital.

Troy had cackled like a witch. Paul had cried with laughter. Jarod had simply smirked at his deranged friends, which was as good as a belly laugh from anyone else.

~

Jarod and Paul sat down on the cushioned wooden loungers and relaxed as the scent of jasmine hung in the air.

"This house is amazing. It's everything I'd ever hoped for and more." Jarod said as he sipped his soda.

"Agreed. Although, I'll be a lot happier once all this unpacking is done. We can finally escape from cardboard box hell and start enjoying our new home."

"Not to worry. All the essentials are complete. All that's really left to do is setting up the library and office downstairs, and then just a little tweaking of the interior design here and there."

"I am not an interior designer. I just put stuff where it fits." Paul snorted.

"Yeah, me too!" Jarod smiled.

"Well, that's why I'm here, boys. I'll make your house gorgeous!" Troy's disembodied voice carried from the other end of the garden.

"I swear he has hearing like a bat…" Paul whispered.

"I heard that!"

"Behave, or I'll make you start alphabetising my books!" Jarod called out. Silence fell from the granny flat. Jarod giggled, "He really does know his stuff. Besides, he couldn't do a worse job than either one of us. Best to leave it to the expert."

"I don't care what the house looks like, as long as I get to come home to you in it," Paul said as he leaned in and kissed Jarod deeply, enjoying the sharp, sweet flavour of the lemon soda on his tongue.

Jarod felt his heart flutter slightly. Once he had figured it had become cold as ice forever. But now basking in Paul's love, his heart was finally unfrozen.

THE END

Don't miss out!

Visit the website below and you can sign up to receive emails whenever Alex Leslie publishes a new book. There's no charge and no obligation.

https://books2read.com/r/B-A-CCJI-DISFB

BOOKS 2 READ

Connecting independent readers to independent writers.

About the Author

Alex Leslie is an Australian-born author of Gay M/M romance works including *Chasing The Cupcake Boy, Following His Bliss* and *My Big Gay Family Christmas Fiasco.*

Alex lives with his partner, two troublesome cats (who love sleeping on his laptop!) and is currently dealing with an ongoing addiction to iced coffee drinks.

Read more at www.alexleslieauthor.com.